Stealing Ronan

ISABEL LUCERO

SOUTH RIVER UNIVERSITY #1
BY
ISABEL LUCERO

Renzo

Chapter One

"WHAT'RE YOU DOING HERE, UGLY?" my sister
Violet asks as she sashays down the hall like it's a fucking
runway.

"I live here, in case you forgot."

She rolls her eyes and flips her blond hair over her shoulder. "I mean, it's Saturday. Why aren't you partying with your
frat bros?" She changes her voice for the last two words, like
she's mocking me.

"First off, I'm not in a frat, so I don't have *frat bros*, and
you know that, and secondly, I don't need to party every
weekend."

She scoffs, making her way through the living room and
to the kitchen where she grabs a bottle of water from the
fridge.

"Well, go find something to do. I have someone coming
over."

I saunter into the kitchen with a grin on my face. "Oh?
Does my baby sister have a boyfriend?"

She grins. "We're...talking."

"Do Mom and Dad know about this guy?"

She looks at me like I'm dumb. "Of course not, and they won't know, because they aren't going to be home until next week."

"Is he spending the night?"

"Ugh. You're so annoying. Go find some guy to jack off or something."

"Nah, I'm good. Already did that earlier," I say, even though it's not true.

Violet pushes past me and starts rearranging the pillows on the couch. "What's the best place to order food from?"

"Well, there's all the pizza places, and a couple Chinese spots."

"I don't really want anything too greasy. Is there a place that delivers like salad or something?"

"Look on DoorDash or something. I'm sure there's a restaurant that serves salad."

"Okay, thanks." She walks up to me, all five foot five of her, and pushes up on her tiptoes to kiss my cheek. "I love you, big brother, but it's time for you to leave."

"I can't believe you're trying to kick me out. Look, I'm not going anywhere, but I'll stay in my room. That cool? I got a couple homework assignments I have to work on anyway."

"Ugh. Fine." She points a finger at me. "Don't be annoying."

"I am older than you, you know."

She laughs. "Dad is older than Mom, and she's still the boss."

"Whatever. I'm going to my room. Don't do anything stupid."

A saccharine sweet smile spreads across her face, but she just waves me off with a few fingers.

In my room, I order a pizza for myself, then sit down at my desk to finish my homework. Before I can even begin, my phone vibrates with a text from my friend Dex.

. . .

I drop my head back with a sigh. Like any twenty-year-old college student, I enjoy my fair share of parties, but me and Trevor have a bit of a past, and unfortunately, it's not that far in the past.

We hooked up at the last party he had two weeks ago, but none of our friends know. Reason why? He's deep in the closet. So much in the closet that when he woke up after our night together, he freaked out and tried to act like he didn't remember what happened. But he knows, because I can see the memories flashing across his eyes when he looks at me.

Shit's awkward as fuck, and I don't feel like being around him right now.

It's not that I haven't been with closeted guys before, because trust me, in college, there's plenty. I don't mind being the one who blows open their world when they realize just how much they love sucking a cock. Hell, I'm all for being the sexual awakening for guys who thought they were straight, but let's be honest. More often than not, way deep down inside, they know. They just don't want to acknowledge or act on it. Probably because of their families. Luckily, I have a great one. I haven't been closeted since I was twelve.

Thirty minutes after I start my work, I get notified that the pizza is being delivered via the app I ordered from, so I get up from the leather chair and leave my room, heading toward the front door.

Violet's head snaps in my direction as soon as she hears my footsteps on the hardwood floor, and her green eyes narrow at me.

"I'm just getting my pizza," I say, holding up my hand, eyeing the bowls of salad on the coffee table. "Where's your boyfriend?"

"Just hurry up and go."

I chuckle, pulling open the door and grabbing the pizza from the delivery guy. "Thanks, man."

"Your guy's okay with eating rabbit food?" I call out, heading to the couch.

"Shut up," she hisses. "He's gonna be out of the bathroom any second."

A noise to my right gets my attention, and the guy my sister's spending time with tonight strolls in, looking exactly like the type of guy I'd love to have some fun with.

He's almost as tall as me, probably just under six feet. I can't see much of his body, but I'd bet he's probably hiding some muscles under that long-sleeved black shirt he's wearing. His hair is short on the sides, but long on the top—long enough for me to be able to tug on. It's styled in a way that you can tell he could run his hand through it, and it would stay perfectly in place.

His face has little facial hair, giving him an innocent vibe, and I've always loved corrupting the innocent.

"Hey," I greet, lifting my chin.

He gives me a nod and smile. "Hey. I'm Ronan."

I take his outstretched hand in mine and shake it. A jolt of desire runs up my arm and into my chest, then down to my cock.

"Renzo."

"Nice to meet you."

Ronan walks past me, parking himself on the couch next to my sister. She shoos me away, widening her eyes and clenching her jaw while mouthing, *go*.

"Hey, man, you want a slice of pizza or something?" I offer, needing to see him a little longer while also pissing my sister off. I jerk my head toward the salads. "Seems like you might need a little more to fill you up."

The statement drips with innuendo, and it takes all my strength to not lick my bottom lip and grin at him, making sure he gets the message.

He looks unsure of what to do, his eyes passing between me and Violet as she struggles to conceal her annoyance.

"Yeah, sure. Thanks. I just came from practice, so I'm starving."

"Practice?" I question.

"Basketball."

My eyes try to peruse his body again, but he's all covered up. "Cool." I open the box and stand behind the couch, letting him reach in to grab one. "Do you go to school with Vi?"

He shakes his head, having already taken a bite. I watch him chew and swallow before he answers. "I'm in college."

I raise a brow, glancing at Violet who's basically fuming. "Is that right? Which college?"

"South River."

My pulse speeds up when I realize he's at the same college I go to, but for whatever reason, I choose not to disclose that. How have I not seen him before? Well, it's a big campus, so it makes sense, but still. He's too hot to not notice.

My sister huffs, taking my attention off Ronan's blue eyes and pink lips. "Well, I guess I'll head back to my room."

"Okay, bye," Violet says right away.

"Take another one," I tell Ronan, gesturing to the pizza. "I won't finish it by myself anyway."

His eyes flicker up at me, baby blue shining between dark lashes, and I can't help but imagine how he'd look up at me if he was on his knees, ready to take my cock. "You sure?"

"Mm." I nod. "Go ahead."

"Thanks, man."

I turn and make my way back to my room, but now I can't focus on my work. All I'm thinking about is what the hell those two are doing out there, and why the universe would send the hottest fucking guy into my life via my sister.

Chapter Two

"WHERE YOU HEADED ALL EARLY on a Sunday?" I ask Violet as she searches for her keys.

"I'm meeting Scarlet and Monique."

"How was your date last night?" I ask for some unknown reason.

"Ugh. You should know since you decided to crash it."

"Please. I was there for like two minutes."

She waves me off, opening kitchen drawers. "Anyway, it was fine."

"How did you meet him if he's in college? Which, I don't really like, by the way."

"What *do* you like?"

"Why would your keys be in the silverware drawer?" I ask.

She stands up straight and raises her arms up. "I don't know! I can't find them."

I lean against the breakfast bar, watching her frantically search for what I'm sure is in the bowl on the table next to the front door. "So, are you going to college parties now, or what?"

"Come on, Zo, this place is a fucking college town. That's all there is."

"I need you to be careful."

"I know, I know."

I sigh. "Check the bowl next to the door. You know, the place we put the keys."

She rushes over and pulls them out, clutching them to her chest as she looks over at me. "You're the best. I'll be back later. Love you!"

The door slams closed before I can even respond.

Me and Vi have always been close. There's only three years between us, and our parents worked a lot while we were growing up. We had nannies, but mostly, we had each other.

Dad was a surgeon and Mom was a pediatrician, and because they adopted us well into their forties, they've recently retired and are now enjoying the ability to travel around. Which means me and Vi have the house to ourselves a lot, and that's why I'm not living on campus. Why have a roommate in a small room when I can have a whole house?

I mentally plan out my day.

First, shower.

Second, eat.

Third, homework.

I was too distracted last night to fully devote my attention to it. All I could think about was how I was stupidly attracted to Violet's kind of boyfriend, hating myself for wanting him even though she has him.

It's not very big brotherly to lust after your sister's boyfriend, but I suppose I need to get over it. He's straight and trying to hook-up with my sister. That's drama I don't need.

After my shower, I pull on a pair of gray sweatpants and run a comb through my brown hair, and then the doorbell rings.

I glance at the oversized clock in our living room as I make my way to the door, noting it's only nine-thirty. Hardly anybody comes over unannounced, especially this early.

When I pull open the door, my eyes connect with the guy who's barely strayed from my thoughts since last night. Ronan.

"Hey," I greet, still holding onto the doorknob as I lean against the open door.

God, he looks even better in the daylight. His full lips—the top one only slightly plumper than the bottom—look pillowy soft. I imagine they'd look fucking amazing wrapped around my cock. His angular jaw and cheekbones make him look like he belongs on a runway, and his skin is flawless.

I don't miss when his baby blues drop to my naked torso. "Sorry," he says quickly. "I know it's early."

"It's fine, but you missed Violet. She left already."

"Oh." He rubs the back of his neck, looking to the side. "I actually didn't come here to see her."

My imagination runs wild, waiting for him to say, *I actually came to see you. I was so drawn to you last night, I had to come by and see you again.* Instead, he says, "I think I dropped my wallet here."

"Oh. Okay. Come in."

I step back and let him inside, closing the door behind him. "You think it's in her room?"

He eyes me, a grin on his lips. "Uh, no. We didn't go to her room last night."

Relief floods me, and I hate it. "So, couch?" I ask, hoping he doesn't sense my happiness.

"Probably."

I gesture for him to check, and then stand nearby, watching him like some sort of creeper. "How old are you?"

His eyes find mine as his hands slide between the cushions. "Nineteen. Why?"

I cross my arms over my chest and shrug. "You're dating my sister. I can ask questions, can't I?"

A tinge of red paints his cheeks. "Yesterday was our first...date."

"Still a date."

He looks up at me again briefly before focusing on the couch, but he doesn't say anything.

"So, what's your position?" I ask.

He coughs. "What?"

I smirk. "You play basketball, right?"

"Oh. Yeah. Point guard."

"So, you're pretty good?"

"I like to think so. What about you? Do you play sports?"

"Does it look like I play sports?"

His eyes dance over my muscles. "Yeah, it does," he says with a chuckle.

"I just like to stay fit, but organized sports ain't my thing. I'll play a game at the park or something, but I don't want the rules."

He finds his wallet and lifts it up to show me before slipping it in his pocket. "So, you're a rule breaker?"

I smile. "You have no idea."

Our eyes stay connected for a couple seconds before he clears his throat. "Well, thanks for letting me in."

"Anytime." I walk him to the door. "Will I see you again?"

He cocks his head slightly. "What do you mean?"

"Will you be visiting my sister again?"

"Oh. Uh, I don't know. Maybe."

"Well, okay. Maybe I'll see you around then."

He steps onto the porch and looks at me over his shoulder. "Yeah. Okay. Take it easy."

"Bye, Ronan."

When his name slips between my lips, I swear his eyes

widen slightly. But then he just walks away, heading to the driveway and into his car.

Fuck. I need to get laid ASAP. I'm fantasizing over a straight dude.

Chapter Three

"DUDE, you missed out on a hell of a party on Saturday," Dex tells me as soon as I walk into the dining hall for lunch. "Trevor was so wasted, he was making out with like three different chicks," he says with a laugh, elbowing Jayden.

"Yeah, man. I've never seen him act like that before," Jay says before taking a bite out of a roll.

He's probably trying to convince himself he doesn't like guys, but I don't bother saying anything. "Ah well, I'll catch the next one. My sister had some guy over, so I had to make sure nothing crazy happened."

"Like what? Her getting laid? You know it's gonna happen eventually," Dex says.

"If it hasn't already," Jayden adds on.

"Gross. Stop," I complain, opening a can of Coke.

"She's seventeen. Almost eighteen. When did you start fucking around?" Dex asks, though he doesn't need to. He knows.

"Shut up," I groan.

"Exactly," he says with a laugh. "But anyway, who is this

guy? Do we need to make it known not to fucking break her heart?"

I chuckle. "Nah, I don't think so. Violet's usually the heartbreaker."

"True," Dex agrees. "That girl is too pretty for her own good."

I cut my eyes to him. "Hey, calm down with that pretty shit. That's my sister."

He laughs, hitting my arm with his. "Dude, come on. I didn't mean it like that."

"Mhm," I mumble before taking a bite of my burger. "Anyway, this dude is what my wet dreams are made out of," I admit.

Jayden nearly spits out his drink, while Dex starts cracking up.

"Excuse me?" Jayden asks.

"You crushing on Violet's boyfriend?" Dex questions.

"He's hot, and he goes here."

"Really? What's his name?" Jayden asks. He knows everybody.

"Ronan. I don't know his last name."

"Hmm." He scratches his chin. "I'll find out soon."

"So, basically. I need to get laid soon before I embarrass myself and come on to him the next time he's over."

"You mean, come on him?" Dex chokes out a laugh.

"You really want to know my sexual prolictivities? Because I'll tell you exactly where I like to come."

Dex pulls a face, shaking his head. "Okay, never mind."

I laugh. "Anyway, so, Trevor was drunk out of his mind, huh?"

"Yeah, man. He asked if you were coming, though."

He probably wanted to make sure I wasn't.

"Speak of the fucking devil," Jayden announces.

I look up and see Trevor heading in our direction. As soon

as he spots me, his steps slow, but he eventually makes it to our table and sits in front of me.

"We were just telling Renzo about your drunken night on Saturday."

Trevor groans, scratching his head. "I don't want to talk about it." He looks at me briefly before focusing on his food.

"Seems like you never want to talk about your drunken hook-ups," I say, unable to help myself.

"Sometimes the alcohol makes me do stupid shit," he replies with a clenched jaw.

I snort. "Anyway, I'm off," I say, standing up. "Gonna go look for a warm mouth to stick my dick in." I glance at everyone at the table, but linger on Trevor. "Unless anyone wants to volunteer."

"Pft. Get the fuck outta here, dude," Dex says with a laugh.

Jayden gives me a fist bump and Trevor avoids my gaze.

After I dump my trash, I travel down the hall, heading for the exit. My next class isn't for another thirty minutes, but I figure I'll stop by the library to do a little research on a project while I have the free time.

But, of course, because the universe is torturing me, I see Ronan at a corner table, huddled over a book. I haven't seen him on campus before, but now, here he is, tempting me.

"You following me?" I ask, dropping into the seat across from him.

His head comes up slowly, like he really doesn't want to pull his eyes from the page. When recognition hits, he grins. "I think I was here first."

"You're right. Maybe I'm following you," I say with a crooked smile.

"So, you go here, too."

"Yep."

There's a few seconds of silence before he speaks again. "Violet invited me over again."

"Oh yeah?" Both jealousy and excitement fill my chest.

"Yeah. She said your parents are still out of town."

"They're overseas."

"Oh. That explains why she was saying there was gonna be a party."

"A what? She's throwing a party?"

He bites down on his lip, and my eyes stay glued to the area for longer than the gesture lasted. "Oops. I guess I shouldn't have said anything."

"I would've found out anyway. I'll talk to her."

"So, no party?" he questions, his blue eyes sparkling as they look at me.

I can't turn down an opportunity to be around him again, even though I should. "Who said that?" I reply with a smirk.

He nods his head, a smile forming. "Then, I guess I'll see you around."

"Yes, you definitely will."

Chapter Four

THE FIRST HALF of the week flies by relatively quickly, with my parents calling to check in on us on Wednesday evening. They're in Italy, enjoying being away from Michigan's cold weather. Meanwhile, I'm freezing my balls off while I wait outside the boutique my sister works at, waiting for her to get off.

"You didn't have to meet me here," she says, wrapping her scarf around her neck.

"I had to park two blocks away, and it's dark. I'm not gonna let you walk two blocks alone."

She nudges me. "Aww. Look at you, caring about me."

I glance down at her and shake my head. "Just try not to wreck your car again, okay? Mom's not gonna wanna let you drive ever again."

"It's only the second time it happened," she says, waving her hand in the air like it's not a big deal.

"For the record, I've never even gotten a ticket."

"Anyway, let's talk about the party. Think we can get alcohol?"

"You are not drinking," I say sternly.

"What?" she screeches. "Why not? I know you and Dex drink all the time."

"First of all, Dex needs to stop telling you shit, and second of all, I'm older than you."

"You're still not old enough to drink, though."

I scoff, and shove my hands deeper into my pockets. "I can't say it's okay for you to drink."

"But?" she questions, peeking up at me with her green eyes, batting her lashes.

"You'll do whatever you're gonna do, but you're gonna keep your ass in the house at all times, and you will not leave my sight."

"Whatever. You'll find some guy to keep your attention and you'll forget all about me."

"Then I'll have Dex watch you."

"Ugh. I don't need Dex babysitting me."

"You're like a sister to him, too. I trust him to make sure you don't do anything stupid."

She goes quiet, stewing in her teenage girl emotions. I wrap my arm around her and pull her in close. "I love you. That's all."

"I know. I love you, too. But you're a cock block."

I gasp. "What? You don't need to know anything about cocks except that they're gross and will give you diseases."

She cackles. "Right, so why do you like them so much?"

I squeeze her a little tighter. "Brat."

"Whatever happened to you and that guy Kris?"

I remove my arm from her shoulder and pull the car keys out to unlock the Jeep Cherokee. "We just broke up," I say with a shrug. "It's been a few months, though. What makes you bring him up?"

Once we're in the car, she answers. "He was nice, and you seemed happy."

"I don't seem happy now?"

She shrugs. "I guess, but it's different."

"Don't worry about it. I'm good. I like being single."

"Me too," she replies with a grin.

"Oh yeah? So, what's up with you and that guy?" I ask, keeping it casual, and purposefully not saying his name.

"Who? Ronan?"

I pull onto the street and nod. "Yeah, him."

"He's cute, right? I don't know. We've just been talking, but I don't know what's gonna happen there."

"I see."

"Why? You don't like him?"

I contemplate my response for a few seconds before I respond. "I like him fine, I guess. I don't really know him."

"Well, he'll be at the party."

In an effort to not think about him, I change the subject. "So, me and Trevor messed around a little."

Violet instantly drops her phone in her purse and shifts to stare at me. I glance over and see her wide eyes and open mouth. "Oh my god! What? Trevor? Trevor Campbell? The Trevor you've known for like six years?"

"That's the one. We were drunk, but not like black out drunk. He freaked out the next day and said he didn't remember what happened, but I seriously doubt that."

"Holy shit, Zo! This is crazy, right? He's straight! Or, at least, I always thought he was."

"Yeah, well, he's not as straight as he wants people to think. I think that's what's freaking him out. He's probably trying to come to terms, but in the meantime, shit is weird between us."

"That sucks. Y'all have been close for a while."

I lift a shoulder. "Well, I don't hate him or anything. I'll try to talk to him this weekend. I invited him to the party. He's still a friend."

"You don't want to pursue that?"

I shake my head. "Nah. I like him, but we'd be better as friends."

"Wow, my mind is blown."

"Just don't tell anybody. He obviously isn't out to anyone."

"Of course. I won't say anything."

The rest of the way to our house, Violet complains about her co-worker and the drama that's going on at work. I don't really know those people, but I let her talk, because I know she needs to vent.

Once we're in the garage, my phone vibrates with a text message. When I pick it up from the center console, I see it's from Jayden.

"I'll be in in a sec," I tell Violet as she rushes in, complaining about needing to pee.

Ronan Caswell. 19. Moved to Michigan a year ago from New Hampshire. Also, who the fuck is from New Hampshire?

I laugh out loud as I shake my head. Leave it to Jayden to actually find out information about this guy. I don't know how he does it, but he knows or can find out just about anything about anybody. It's almost scary.

How in the hell did you find out where he's from?

I got connections. ;)

One day you're gonna have to tell me what they are, but thanks. I don't think I'll be trying anything with him, anyway. He likes Vi, and, you know, vaginas. So, I'm out.

You never know...

The fact that he lets that trail off piques my interest, but I decide to leave it alone. I need to stop being excited about seeing him on Saturday. Maybe I'll invite one of my past conquests. I need someone to focus my pent up sexual energy on, and it can't be Ronan Caswell from New Hampshire.

Chapter Five

JUST LIKE THAT, it's Saturday, and our house is teeming with people. It's mostly Violet's friends, but I made sure to invite Trevor, Dex, and Jayden just so I wasn't surrounded by seventeen and eighteen-year-old girls.

We all started out in the living room and kitchen area, but me and the guys eventually moved into the basement where we have a pool table, black leather couch, and a seventy-five-inch TV mounted on the wall. It's supposed to be my dad's "Man-Cave" but he rarely comes down here anymore.

Every once in a while, me or Dex go upstairs to check things out, but so far there's only two guys here, and the girls Violet invited over don't seem to be showing them too much attention.

Down in the basement, we have a mini-fridge stocked with beer, and my dad has a mini-bar with a good amount of liquor, so I just try to remember what I need to replace as we drain the beers and sip out of the bottles of hard stuff.

We let a game of pool distract us for a little while, and then when I realize I haven't been upstairs in quite some time, I jog up the steps prepared to either see a raging party, or for

Violet to be gone. Luckily, neither's the case, but there are a few more people here, including Ronan.

I spot a couple other guys holding beer bottles, so I'm assuming someone brought them over. Then I see Violet taking a sip out of a beer can, pulling the most sour face possible. Ronan laughs at her, reaching out to brush her hair out of her face. Jealousy grows in my stomach, but it's quickly stomped out by annoyance. Not at them, but at myself for even being jealous in the first place.

I clear my throat as I approach, raising my eyebrows at Violet.

"Hey, Zo. You remember Ronan?" she asks, gesturing toward him while trying to hide the beer can with her other hand.

My eyes do a slow perusal from Ronan's eyes, all the way down to his feet. Dressed in a pair of chinos and a light blue, long sleeved button up with a navy blue sweater over it, he looks like a prep school kid, and it makes my dick twitch. "Yes, I remember. Hi, Ronan. So, you're drinking beer," I state, quickly turning my attention to Vi.

"What?" she squeals, playing dumb.

"I already saw you, so there's no point in lying. Based on the face you made, you probably won't want more than one, but don't drink more than two." I face Ronan who's already watching me. "You gonna keep an eye on her?"

"Oh, yeah. Of course."

Violet scoffs. "I'm right here, and I'm fully capable of taking care of myself."

"Okay, well, I'll be downstairs."

"So, Ronan, you were telling me about your cock," Violet says as I'm turning away.

I spin back around and narrow my eyes at Ronan who stammers over his words, his eyes growing in size. "Uh, no. No, I didn't—"

Violet cracks up. "I'm kidding, jeez!" She turns around and starts talking to one of her friends.

Ronan exhales. "I wouldn't tell her about...you know."

My lips curl up on one side. "Your cock?"

"Right."

Despite knowing better, I step closer and lean against the counter, watching him closely. "You can't say cock?"

"Of course I can say cock." He emphasizes the last word, sending dirty thoughts bouncing through my mind.

My tongue swipes across my bottom lip as my eyes watch his mouth. "Mm." It's nearly a groan, but hopefully he didn't hear it that way.

"So, you're not telling my sister about your dick, but you're trying to give it to her?"

He shifts uncomfortably. "No, man. What? I'm not talking about this."

As much as I want to continue standing here talking to him, I know I'm wasting my time. "Okay. See ya around."

I head back down to the basement and open a fresh beer, hoping I can drown out the thoughts of Ronan and his pretty fucking mouth.

Twenty minutes later, after Jay and Dex finish another game of pool, they head upstairs to grab some food, leaving me and Trevor alone.

I swallow down the rest of my beer and walk toward him so I can toss it in the trash.

"Hey."

Trevor's probably as tipsy as me. I can see it in his eyes. "Hey."

"I think we should talk."

He snorts. "Sounds like you're about to break up with me or something."

"You remember, don't you?" I ask, going straight to the point.

He sighs, gazing down at his feet. "Yeah."

"Do you blame me? You think I forced you or something?"

His head snaps up, his eyes meeting mine. "No, no. Of course not." He runs a hand through his hair. "God. I'm sorry. It's just..." he trails off, focusing his gaze on his hands as he nervously cracks his knuckles.

"Confusing?" I offer.

He laughs a short, humorless laugh. "You could say that. I thought I was straight. I've been with girls my whole life."

"Maybe you're bi," I say with a shrug.

His mouth twists up. "I don't know."

"Well, for what it's worth, you're pretty good."

Trevor laughs. "*Pretty* good?"

"I've had better," I tease.

He elbows me. "Dick."

"Yes, you suck dick pretty good."

Trevor stands up straight, turning to face me, his teeth digging into his bottom lip. Before I know it's going to happen, he presses his mouth to mine.

He slips his tongue between my lips, and the alcohol, plus extreme horniness takes over, and I pull him into me and take control. I take over the kiss, plunging my tongue into his mouth while gripping the back of his neck.

I only let it go on for a few more seconds before I pull away. "Fuck."

He wipes his mouth with his hand. "Yeah, well, I'm definitely into dudes."

I laugh, shaking my head. "I think we should keep our relationship as friends. As much as I like kissing you, it's probably for the best to not let this go any further."

He nods. "Yeah, you're probably right." Trevor touches his cock through his jeans. "I'm gonna go to the bathroom. Not to jack off. Just to adjust."

"Right," I say with a laugh.

"We're good, though?" he questions.

"We're good."

He struts off, and when he closes the door behind him, I turn and find Ronan watching me from the bottom of the stairs.

"Hey," I greet softly, wondering how much he saw.

He snaps out of his daze by literally shaking his head. "Sorry. Um." He looks back up the stairs, pointing. "Violet said I could use the bathroom down here since the one up there is full of girls, and she doesn't want anyone upstairs."

"Yeah, sure. My friend just went in there, but you can use it after him."

"Cool. Thanks."

He stays where he is, like he's afraid to come any closer. "So, how much did you see?" I question.

"I didn't see anything." He says it too quickly in a tone too high. He's lying.

I study his face carefully before I walk in his direction. I get as close as possible without touching him, then angle my head down so my mouth is positioned right by his ear.

"Your *cock* says otherwise. That's interesting."

Before he can respond, I walk upstairs, because lord knows all I want to do is bend him over and bury myself deep inside him. Just because the erection he started sporting was visible behind the light-colored pants he has on doesn't mean anything. I haven't gotten laid in weeks, so I think I'd be turned on by anything. Maybe it's been a while for him, too.

Chapter Six

"HEY, MY BABIES," Mom greets when she walks through the door.

Mom's short blond hair is mixed with gray, but perfectly in place as usual. Though she's in her sixties, she'll tell you she's in her fifties, but she can definitely pull off the lie.

Me and Vi get up from the couch and give her a hug. "Hey, Mom. How was it?" I ask.

"Beautiful. Absolutely beautiful. But I missed you two."

"Even him?" Vi asks, jerking her thumb at me.

"I know, right?" Mom replies with a conspiratorial whisper, winking at Violet.

"We all know I'm the favorite anyway."

Violet rolls her eyes, then eyes a necklace my mom's wearing. "Oh my God! That's beautiful!"

"You like it?" Mom asks.

"I love it."

"Good, because I got one for you, too."

Violet squeals and I shake my head. "Where's Dad?"

"Getting the bags."

"I'll help him."

"We got you something, too," she says as I'm walking toward the garage door.

"Is it a trip to Italy?" I joke.

"You wish."

"Hey, Dad. Need help?"

Dad glances at me over his shoulder as he pulls a Coach suitcase out of the trunk. "Yeah, sure. Your mom bought half of Italy, so we had to buy new luggage to accommodate all the souvenirs."

My father, a man who's closer to seventy than sixty, is still in decent shape himself. They've both dedicated time to their daily walks, and eat better than anyone I've known. Regardless of their healthy habits, age has weighed them down a little, but you can only tell by their early bedtimes, midday naps, and few complaints of aching joints.

I yank out two suitcases and place them on the garage floor. "Well, did you have a good time?"

"Yes, it was great. The food was phenomenal," he says, patting his stomach.

"The food here was also phenomenal. We had pizza and Chinese a lot."

He purses his lips at me. "You'll regret that when you wake up at thirty and gain fifteen pounds overnight."

"Oh, is that how it works, Doctor?" I say with a laugh.

"Smartass," he murmurs. "Did your mother tell you her plans?"

"No."

"For Christmas break, she wants us to go to Sleeping Bear Dunes. She said you and Vi can invite a friend to come along."

"Hmm. Okay," I say with a shrug. "Might be fun."

"Yeah, it's about a two hour drive, though. We'll figure out the logistics later, but invite a friend."

"Okay. Thanks."

After we bring the luggage in and lug it upstairs into their room, they both decide to take a nap, and I go back down to talk to Violet.

"Did Mom tell you about the Christmas trip?" I ask.

"Yeah. Sleeping Bear? It's gonna be cold as fuck, though."

"Yeah, but we can ski or go sledding. Who you gonna bring?"

"I'm not sure. She said one friend. If I choose Monique over Scarlet, then Scarlet's gonna be pissed, but if I choose Scarlet over Monique—"

"Let me guess, she'll be pissed?"

"Right. So, I don't know. Who are you bringing?"

I think about it for a sec. "Probably Dex."

"That easy, huh?"

"Pretty much."

"Whatever. I'll figure it out when the time comes." She stands up. "I gotta go get ready. Ronan's probably on his way right now."

"Ronan's coming over?" My voice sounds too excited, so I tone it down. "Y'all have a date or something?"

"Or something," she says cheekily before rushing off to her room.

I stretch my arms out across the back of the couch, letting my head drop back against the soft, ivory-colored cushion. My eyes are only closed for what feels like a few seconds before the doorbell rings.

"Get that, Zo!" Violet yells. "Keep him company until I'm ready."

I groan, pushing up from the couch. "Fine, but hurry up. I'm not a babysitter." I don't bother adding that it's because I don't trust myself to be around him long. Not that I'll force myself on him, but my tongue is as wicked as it is talented, and I'm bound to confess my attraction without even trying to.

I pull open the door to find a very attractive Ronan on my

porch once again. The cold wind blows his hair in all directions, and his cheeks and the tip of his nose are already turning red. "Hey, come in," I say. "She's still getting ready."

He rubs his hands together, trying to warm them up as he steps inside. "Thanks. It's so fucking cold today."

"Yeah, they're saying it's probably gonna snow soon."

We both go straight for the couch, sitting on each end and staring up at the TV that's mounted above the fireplace. Silently, we watch a couple commercials before reruns of The Office come on.

"So, where are you two headed tonight?" I question, needing to fill the silence.

"Just to go eat," he answers, before quickly adding, "There's a group of us."

I don't respond, and the awkwardness between us is thick. He's probably thinking about last weekend when he watched me and Trevor make out, and all I'm thinking about is how I want to stick my tongue down his throat.

I cut my eyes to him when he shifts, unzipping his jacket.

"She's probably gonna be a little while. You might as well take it off and get comfortable."

He wordlessly stands up and peels off the gray Peacoat that makes him look like a preppy runway model. I unabashedly watch him, and he meets my gaze, staring down at me as he lays it carefully over the back of the couch.

He sits down, rubs his palms over his jeans, and looks in my direction. "So, was that your boyfriend?"

I arch a brow and cock my head at him. "No, I don't have a boyfriend."

"Oh. Sorry, I didn't mean to—"

"Ask about my personal life?"

"Just trying to have a conversation."

I laugh. "No worries, man. I'm just fucking with you. I'm an open book. What else do you want to know?"

He fights off a smile, sliding his eyes in my direction before looking back at the TV. "You make me uncomfortable."

"What? Why?" I ask, sitting up and facing him.

He laughs. "I just never know what to expect from you."

"What do you mean?"

After a few beats, he says, "Sometimes I think you hate me, and other times, I think you're trying to be cool."

"Well, you throw me off my game, I guess."

He studies me, trying to figure out what I mean. Hell, I don't even know. This guy has me so worked up. I hate that he's always here, but only because he's not here for me. I hate that I want him as bad as I do. He's just reading my mood swings.

"I don't even know what that means," he says with a chuckle.

"Hell, I don't either. Never mind."

Ronan laughs again. "Okay."

"I like you," I tell him, making his head angle in my direction. "I mean, I don't hate you, so don't worry about that."

"Oh. Okay. Cool."

I roll my eyes at myself. This shit is stupid. Why am I even sitting here talking to him?

I stand up and look down at him. "I'm gonna head out. Guess I'll see ya around."

"Yeah. Okay," he replies, those damn baby blues piercing my soul as he gazes up at me.

"Violet, I'm leaving. Hurry up," I yell before grabbing my coat and keys and storming out of the house.

Chapter Seven

I END up meeting Jayden at Nicola's pizza parlor, grateful that he wasn't doing shit either.

We bump fists before I sit down across from him. "I invited my friend to meet us here. You haven't met him, but he's cool," he says.

I nod. "All right. I just needed to get out of the house."

"What's going on?" he asks, putting his phone down.

"Nothing serious. I'm just a horny fucking idiot."

Jayden chokes out a laugh. "Aren't we all?"

I grin. "I guess so."

He scratches the stubble across his chin. "This about that kid?"

"You mean Ronan Caswell from New Hampshire?" I inquire with a smirk.

"Hey, that's just the basics," he says. "I can get you a two page rundown on the kid."

I shake my head. "I'm glad you already know everything about me, otherwise I'd be afraid of what you'd find out."

"Yeah, you're an open book. Boring. I like the hard cases."

"How do you find out all these things?"

"I told you. Connections. I know everybody, and everybody has something to say about someone else. I just use my charms."

I roll my eyes and shake my head. Though, he's not lying. Jayden's liked by everybody. It's almost weird.

"Anyway, yeah. He was at the house before I left. He's going out with Violet again, but she wanted me to stay downstairs and talk to him while she got ready." I run my hand over my face. "I just want to flirt with him all the time. Which is stupid."

"Because he's straight?"

"No, because he's with my sister."

"Wouldn't him being straight kind of be a problem?" he asks with a deep chuckle.

"Yeah, but flirting with a straight guy wouldn't make me feel like shit. Flirting with someone my sister likes makes me feel like an asshole."

"Well, you kinda are."

"Not a *steal my sister's boyfriend* kind of asshole."

"That's assuming he'd let you steal him."

"Ugh. Shut up."

Jayden laughs, then our waiter finally makes his way over and takes our order. A few minutes later we get our drinks, and I practically beg Jayden to tell me anything about his life to take my mind off my fucked up situation.

"I'm kinda crushing on two people right now," he says.

"Wow, calm down with these crazy confessions," I deadpan.

"Fuck off," he says with a laugh.

"All right, who are these people? Are they guys? Girls? One of each?"

Jayden came out as bisexual last year.

He rubs the back of his neck, and I lean in, wanting to know who they are.

"Well, actually…"

"Hey, sorry I'm late," a guy says as he approaches the table.

I'm ready to be annoyed that he interrupted Jayden's juicy story, but he's cute. Really cute.

"No worries," Jayden says, scooting over and making room for him. "This is Renzo."

I lift my chin. "Hey."

"Hey. I'm Bryant."

"Bryant's new," Jayden offers.

"Well, I was born and raised around here. If you need anything, let me know," I say with a smile.

Out of the corner of my eye, I see Jayden shaking his head, hiding a smile.

About ten minutes later, as our food gets to the table, Jayden's eyes widen as he notices something behind me.

"What?" I turn around and spot Violet and Ronan walk in, surrounded by four other people. Looks like a triple date. "Of fucking course they're here."

"Who's that?" Bryant asks.

"His sister and the guy he's madly in love with, AKA his sister's boyfriend."

Bryant's eyes bulge.

"Thanks for that," I tell Jayden. "Anyway, it's not that serious. I think he's cute. So, sue me. I'm not fucking him, nor am I madly in love."

As I'm shoving more pizza in my mouth, Violet and her crew are seated at the table next to us. I meet Jayden's gaze and he starts cracking up, getting a kick out of my misery.

"Renzo?" Violet questions. I turn my head and force a smile, nodding since my mouth is full. "Oh, hey, Jay," she adds.

"Hey, Vi. How you been, girl?"

She smiles wide. "I'm doing great."

"This your boyfriend?" Jayden asks, gesturing to Ronan while slyly cutting his eyes to me.

I want to kill him.

"Oh," Vi giggles. "We're just...friends." The *for now* is implied. "Oh shoot. I left my purse in the car. Can I get the keys?" she asks Ronan.

Once she leaves the table, the rest of her crew talk amongst themselves, but Jayden continues to torture me.

"Ronan, right?" Jayden asks.

Ronan looks at him. "Yeah."

Jayden's lips curl up as he very obviously stares at me before focusing on Ronan again. "Yeah, I've heard a little about you."

Poor Ronan looks confused, but plays it off with a smile. He probably thinks I've just been talking shit about him. Honestly, I hope that's what he thinks and not anything else.

I kick Jayden under the table, and he finally leaves it alone. I decide to spend the rest of the time focusing on Bryant. He's cute and he doesn't seem to mind my flirty statements.

"What's your story, Bryant?" I ask. "Single or got a girlfriend?"

He smirks, amused at my way of trying to figure out if he's straight. "Single. No boyfriend."

"Is that right?" I ask, my smile growing.

Jayden groans, making me laugh. I happen to glance to my right and see Ronan watching me with parted lips. Fuck, I want to be in his mouth so bad. I want to explore it with my tongue and ravish it with my cock.

I lick my lips as I stare at his mouth, envisioning all the things I want to do, then I finally lift my gaze and meet his eyes. I wink at him before turning back to Bryant.

"Wanna get outta here?" I ask. "That cool, Jayden? You probably got a couple people to see," I joke.

Jayden raises his hand slowly and gives me the finger with

a fake smile plastered on his face. "Just go. I actually do have plans," he says, lifting his phone.

I raise my eyebrows at Bryant in question, and he nods. "Yeah, let's go."

I throw a twenty on the table to cover half of the bill and knock my fist against Jayden's. "Thanks, bro. I'll talk to you later."

"Yep. Have fun." His light brown eyes twinkle with amusement.

I catch Ronan's eye right before I drape my arm over Bryant's shoulder and walk out. For someone who's straight, he sure does like looking at me, and I'm not gonna lie, I enjoy having his attention.

Chapter Eight

I END up spending a little over an hour with Bryant after leaving the pizza parlor. He hopped in my car with me, and we drove out to Lake Renap, and I pulled up as close to the water as possible. It's surrounded by trees, giving you the security of seclusion, and since nobody else was out there, we had the place to ourselves.

After chatting for about fifteen minutes, he sucked my dick and I jacked him off. Not the greatest sexual experience, but a release is a release, and his mouth is better than my hand. But I'd be lying if I said I didn't think about Ronan the whole time, because I did. I closed my eyes tight and imagined it was his hair I was gripping, and that it was his mouth I was sinking into.

After I drove him back to his car, we exchanged numbers and parted ways with a half-baked plan to maybe meet up again.

Now, as I pull into my driveway, I wish I would've just stayed out, because Ronan's car is parked in the driveway. Is he trying to torture me on purpose?

I walk in and throw my keys in the bowl on the entryway table, ready to bypass them and head straight to my room.

"Renzo, have you met Ronan?" my mom asks.

My eyes dart to the living room where I'm surprised to see my mom and dad sitting on the couch while Ronan and Violet sit on the loveseat opposite them. He's meeting our parents already?

"Yeah, they've met," Violet answers.

I stick my hands in my pockets and walk a little closer. "Yeah, we've bumped into each other a few times."

"Why don't you join us?" Mom asks, patting the cushion next to her with a smile on her face.

I open my mouth to politely decline, but Vi speaks up first. "Who was that guy you were with at the restaurant? New boyfriend? He's cute."

My mom gasps. "Oh, do you have a boyfriend? Come tell us about him. What's his name?"

I drop my head back and groan. "He's not a boyfriend. I just met him. He's friends with Jayden."

"How is Jayden?" Dad asks. "I can't wait to see him on the football field again."

My dad is a huge football fan, and goes to every college game he can. "He's doing pretty good."

"Good, good," he replies with a double nod.

"So, Ronan," my mom says, turning her attention to him. "Do you have plans for Christmas? Are you going home?"

He clears his throat. "No, ma'am. I'll be staying here."

Mom tilts her head, her lips pulling into a slight frown. I already know where this is going, and there's nothing I can do to stop it.

"Well, we're heading up to Sleeping Bear, and you're welcome to join us. You'll stay in your own room, of course," she says with a grin.

Violet perks up, her smile growing as she sits straighter.

"Yes, that would be great!" she says, grabbing onto his bicep. "Please come. It'll be so much fun."

I watch closely as his eyes dart from my mom's, to dad's, and then to Violet's. He looks a little nervous, if not uncomfortable. He probably doesn't like to be put on the spot.

"He might have work to do or something," I say, giving him an out. Not only for his sake, but for mine. I can't imagine being holed up in a cabin with him for two weeks.

Ronan's eyes find mine, and for a few long seconds, I wonder what's running through his mind, but my mom speaks up.

"Well, yes, of course. No pressure, Ronan. You just let Violet know."

He gives her a tight smile and nods.

"Well, I'm heading to my room," I say, turning on my heel and walking away.

"Zo, hold up," Vi calls, coming after me.

I keep going, disappearing into the hallway so we won't be watched by everyone else.

"You're already introducing him to Mom and Dad?" I ask right away.

She scrunches her face. "No, they were in the garage when he pulled up to drop me off, so you know Mom had to invite him in to meet him. You know how she is. She likes to know everybody I hang out with."

"And now you want him to come on vacation with us? You haven't even known him that long."

She crosses her arms. "Why are you being a dick? Do you not like him?"

"I don't fucking know him, and neither do you."

"You're such an asshole," she bites. "I don't know why you care so much."

I know why, but I can't tell her. So now I just get to look like a prick for no reason.

I sigh. "What did you want?"

"Just forget it," she says with a huff, spinning around and stomping off.

Closing my eyes, I let the back of my head hit the wall and blow out a long breath. Footsteps have my eyes popping open, and Ronan rounds the corner, stopping short when he sees me.

"Of course it's you," I say, unable to filter my thoughts before they leave my mouth.

He jolts back a little, surprised by my words. "Uh."

I push away from the wall and step toe-to-toe with him. To his credit, he doesn't back away, just angles his head slightly to maintain eye contact.

Fuck, he's sexy. I'm lost in his eyes for a while, studying how the dark blue outer edge of his irises meld into a softer blue. Then there's his mouth. Those lips. So pink, so pouty, and so inviting.

When I realize I can feel his body against mine, I glance down and notice the heaving of his chest. His breaths are so deep, his chest touches mine with every inhale.

It's then that I stop studying how hot he looks, and start noticing how he's looking at me.

I cock my head. "Ronan." It comes out like a question, and I eagerly await a response I'm dying for, but won't get.

His tongue darts across his bottom lip before he opens his mouth to reply. He presses his lips together and then tries again. "I was gonna go to the bathroom."

I stay quiet for a couple seconds. "I see."

He steps around me before turning back and saying, "Do you not want me to go with you guys to Sleeping Bear?"

I debate my answer. I nearly bite my tongue off to keep from saying the truth, but it comes out anyway. "No. I want you to come, and that's probably why you shouldn't."

Chapter Nine

TWO AND A HALF WEEKS LATER, over a foot of snow has fallen, and we're getting ready to head to Sleeping Bear Dunes.

I've seen Ronan a few times in those seventeen days, but I've been sure to keep my distance. We haven't spoken to each other since that moment in the hallway, and I've done my best to keep from thinking about him at all.

"Dude, I'm so fucking stoked to get away for two weeks," Dex says from the passenger seat in my Jeep.

"It's not like we're going far."

"Yeah, but we're gonna be able to ski and shit. Plus, you know I smuggled some alcohol in my bag. Thank fuck your parents got us different cabins."

"Yeah, they don't want to be kept up by us loud mouths," I say with a laugh. "Mom said their cabin is probably twenty minutes away."

"And we're staying with Vi and her boyfriend?" he questions.

"I fucking guess. But of course Mom and Dad don't want

her and him staying together alone, so we have to be there to watch them."

"I don't want to watch shit," he gripes.

"You're telling me."

"You still got a thing for this guy?"

"Do I still think he's hot as fuck? Yes. Will anything come of it? No."

"Why couldn't she bring a girlfriend?" Dex asks.

"She could only pick one and didn't want to cause drama, so this was the easy way out."

"Easy for who?"

I scoff. "Yeah, not me."

An hour later, we're all at the cabin my mom and dad got for themselves, having already checked into ours. We went in, looked around, turned on the heater, and then came here to have dinner together.

Mom and Dad packed both mine and their own car with food that could stand being out of the fridge during our drive, but also stopped at a small grocery store when we got in town to buy a few more things. Tomorrow, we'll have to head back to the store to stock up on more food, but in the meantime, Mom starts a huge pot of chili and makes a pan of cornbread.

Me and Dex tour their cabin, which is way too big for just the two of them, and end up finding a room with a pool table and foosball.

"That dude's pretty quiet," Dex says, grabbing a pool stick.

"Yeah," I agree. "I don't know why he came. He's probably uncomfortable around all of us."

Someone clears their throat, so I look up from racking the balls and find Ronan at the door.

"Care if I join?" he questions.

Dex rolls his eyes at me, making me grin. "Yeah, that's fine."

"Where's Vi?" Dex asks him.

"Her mom wanted her to help her cook. I felt like maybe she just wanted to talk to her, so I left."

"She's probably telling her not to do anything stupid with you while we're here," I say, stepping back from the table and extending the pool stick to him.

Ronan takes it from me. "I wouldn't do that."

Dex snorts. "If I was at a cabin with a chick, you bet your ass I'd be doing something. More like, everything."

Ronan bends over the table, lining up his shot, and putting his ass directly in my view. "Maybe I'm more respectful than you," he tells Dex without looking at him.

I raise a brow at my friend, a grin growing.

"Maybe you're just a pussy," Dex snips.

Ronan sends the white ball flying into the rest, breaking it beautifully, the balls scattering across the table with a couple dropping into the pockets. He walks around the table, figuring out his next shot.

"Maybe you're jealous," Ronan states, sending another stripe into a pocket.

"Jealous of what?" Dex questions, his brows furrowing.

"That you're not here with a girl," Ronan replies, unruffled by Dex's obvious annoyance. "Unless you and Renzo have a thing going on."

Fully amused, I smile wide and meet Dex's eyes.

"Fuck off. I'm not into dudes. No offense, Zo. I love you, man. But not like that."

"Your loss," I say, winking at him.

Dex shakes his head and Ronan lines up another shot.

"Anyway, you better not try anything with Violet," Dex threatens.

"I thought I was a pussy for not trying anything," Ronan quips with a slight grin.

Dex shifts. "Yeah, well, me and Zo are in the same cabin, so we'll make sure nothing's going on."

Ronan sinks another shot and my brows shoot up in amazement.

"You gonna sleep in my bed with me?" Ronan questions. "Or hers?"

"Nobody's sleeping in her bed," I chime in. "But if you're looking for company..."

Dex coughs to cover his laugh, but Ronan doesn't react. Instead, he misses the ball he was aiming for. Well, I affected him in some way.

"From what I remember, you didn't want me to come," Ronan says from the other side of the table.

Dex ignores us, trying to figure out his shot.

"You're remembering it wrong."

We stay locked in on each other for several seconds before Violet pops in the doorway.

"Dinner will be ready in twenty minutes."

I continue to stare at Ronan, but he looks away first, seeking Vi's face. "Okay. Wanna walk around outside first? Check out the area?"

She makes a face. "It's snowing."

"Vi, we're gonna be up here for two weeks. It's December. Of course it's snowing. It's going to snow pretty often. Are you never gonna leave the cabin?" I ask.

"There's plenty to do inside," she says, aiming a grin at Ronan.

Dex makes a noise and Violet shoots him a dirty look.

"Let me finish this game and I'll go find you," Ronan says.

"Okay," she chirps.

It doesn't take long to finish the game. Dex makes one

ball, misses the next, and then Ronan sinks the rest of his, including the eight ball. He places his stick on the table and smirks at Dex before leaving.

"I hate that guy," Dex complains.

I laugh. "I wish I could say the same."

Chapter Ten

AS WE EAT, the wind picks up outside, battering against the windows.

"Goodness, sounds bad out there," Mom exclaims.

"I think we should head to our cabin soon," Violet says. "We have to drive twenty minutes to get to ours, and I hate driving in bad weather."

"You aren't driving anywhere," Dad says. "Your driving is questionable in good conditions."

"Hey!" she squeals, faux pouting.

Dad finishes his bowl of chili before taking the empty dish to the kitchen. "Actually, maybe you all should stay here. Me and your mom can drive out to the other cabin."

"Well, it's also not safe for you to be driving either," I say.

"I'm well-trained to drive in a snowstorm," Dad says with confidence. Mom rolls her eyes.

"How are you trained?" I question.

"Okay, fine, our vehicle is better equipped."

Mom gets up and washes her dishes. "Your father is right. We don't need this huge space anyway. Plus, you all can use that little game room. We won't use it. The other cabin is still spacious, but this is definitely bigger, and there's more of you."

"Well, let me follow you up there," I say, pushing away from the table.

"Don't be silly," Mom replies, waving me off.

"I left my phone charger and makeup bag over there," Vi complains. "I need that stuff."

"You don't *need* it," I say.

"Shut up. You don't get it." She looks at Mom. "I have some *other* stuff there that I need."

Based on the wide eyes she sends my mom, and the knowing nod my mom gives in response, I can assume she's talking about womanly things that I'm grateful I never have to worry about.

"Well, let's hurry up and go, so we can get you back before the weather is too bad," Mom says.

"Mom, I'll drive her, so you don't have to drive back here," I say.

"No, it's fine, I'll take her," Dex says, sending me a look like he's doing me a favor. He most definitely is not.

"No, I'll do it," I say through clenched teeth and a fake smile. "Let me just go to the bathroom first."

I rinse my bowl out and drop it in the dishwasher before going to the bathroom. After I'm done, I head back to the room with the pool table, knowing I left my keys on one of the tables in there. When I don't find them, I head back to the living room and find my mom and dad walking out the front door.

"I can't find my keys," I tell them. "Give me a minute."

"Dex has them," Mom says, tilting her head. "He said you changed your mind. He and Violet are already in the car."

As patiently as I can, I wait for my dad to help my mom down the stairs, when all I want to do is push past them and yank Dex out of the car so I'm not left with Ronan. I step onto the porch, sans jacket, the wind and snow whipping across my face. I point a finger at Dex through the passenger window, mouthing threats, only to be met by laughter. I can't hear him, but he's definitely cracking up.

He pulls off before I can do anything about it. Fucking asshole.

"Honey, go back inside, you'll catch a cold," Mom scolds.

"I'll call when we get there," Dad says, helping Mom in the car.

"Be careful."

I rush back inside, slamming the door, and shaking the snow from my hair.

Ronan stands in the kitchen, his hip leaning against the counter. "Wanna play pool?" he asks with a cocky grin.

"You think you can whoop my ass?"

He grins. "Scared?"

"You haven't seen me play. You don't know how good I am."

"Or how bad."

"Just because you beat Dex doesn't mean you can beat me."

"Then put your money where your mouth is."

I wet my bottom lip, wanting to make a comment about where I'd rather my mouth be, but I hold it back.

"Let's go, pretty boy."

He chuckles but follows me as I head to the pool room.

"Let's make this interesting," I say.

"How so? You wanna bet?"

"For every ball I sink, you have to answer a question."

He hesitates. "And for every ball I make?"

"What do you want?"

"I guess the same."

"Deal. Wanna break?"

"I'll let you go first."

I smirk. "Such a gentleman."

Just as I'm about to send the white ball into the rest, Ronan steps up to the table, his crotch coming right into view. The balls scatter, but not very well. I don't make a single one.

I stand up straight and study him. He doesn't grin or laugh, so maybe it was just a coincidence. He couldn't have tried to distract me on purpose, right?

He slowly rounds the table, studying it from every angle, while I study the angles of his face.

"Take it easy on me," I say as he bends at the waist, not talking about the game at all.

His head slowly turns in my direction, the corner of his lips drawing up on one side. "Didn't take you for someone who wanted anything easy."

I laugh. "I think you're getting to know me pretty well already."

Of course he sends the blue solid straight into a pocket. He stands up, looking smug as he grips the stick in his hand, grinning at me.

"Whatever, what's your question?" I ask.

He mulls it over for a little while. "When did you know you were gay?"

My eyebrows shoot up as my eyes widen a little. Out of everything he could've asked, I didn't expect this.

"Well, it was pretty early. Probably ten or eleven."

He nods, accepting the answer, then moves to the other side of the table. The red ball drops into the pocket.

"What do you do for fun?"

I snort. "You really want to know?"

He makes a face. "There has to be something else besides sex."

"Sex is fun, though."

He continues to stare at me, so I give in. "Fine, but don't laugh."

Ronan's full lips pull into a small grin. "I'm really curious now."

"I like to rent a canoe and go out in the water.

"Oh. I thought it was gonna be bad, like racing ferrets or something."

"Racing ferrets?" I say with a laugh. "Do people do that?"

"Yep. Why do you think canoeing is embarrassing?"

"That's another question," I say with a wink.

Truth of the matter is I don't think it is embarrassing, but most everyone knows me as the life of the party, the loud, talkative extrovert, but sometimes I just want to get away from everything and enjoy the silence that being in the middle of a lake alone can offer.

He walks toward me, angling his body over the corner of the table, and glances back at me to make sure he's not gonna hit me. I decide to step up behind him, steering clear of the stick and staying on the other side. I peek over his shoulder to see which ball he's aiming for.

I let my right foot rest just inside his left, my leg barely brushing against his. "You're not gonna make that."

Ronan stiffens, glancing back at me. I smirk at him and move to his side, not touching him, but still close.

"How'd you get so good at playing with balls?" I ask just as he takes his shot.

He sputters out a laugh, falling over the table, completely missing the ball. "Fuckin' cheater."

I chuckle and move around the table. "Just an innocent question."

"Yeah, well, you haven't made one yet, so you don't get to ask any questions."

After lining up my shot, I send the white ball into the yellow stripe, and it goes right in the pocket. I stand up and grin. "Hmm. What's my first question gonna be?" I muse, tapping on my chin. "How'd you meet my sister?"

"At a party. I was hanging out with a couple friends, and when they left to get another drink, she approached me."

"Hmm." I make another shot. "Are you close with your family?"

"The fact that I'm here with you guys on Christmas break should answer that."

I make the next shot. "When was the last time you had a girlfriend?"

He shifts, switching the stick to his other hand. "I haven't...I mean, I don't really know. I guess it's been a while."

Unfortunately, I miss the next shot, but he makes his.

"What's your biggest regret?"

After thinking it over for a few seconds, I say, "I don't have any, but I have a feeling one's coming."

He cocks his head, curious, but knows he can't ask another question yet.

Fortunately for me, he misses. When I make mine, I keep it simple.

"What's your favorite kind of ice cream?"

He chuckles, ducking his head. "Don't laugh." I arch a brow. "Vanilla, but it has to have sprinkles."

"Sprinkles?" I question.

"Rainbow sprinkles. It's always been my favorite. I know, it's boring."

"I kind of like that your favorite ice cream is so boring. It's better than liking something like pineapple cilantro or goat cheese beet swirl."

He pulls a face. "What? Those can't be real flavors."

"They really are. I read an article on some of the strangest flavors of ice cream. There's another place that mixes what could be normal flavors, like orange, mango, and strawberry, but they add a scorpion on the top."

"Gross."

"Yeah, so vanilla and sprinkles isn't too bad."

We go back and forth, sticking to easy, simple questions, until the last three balls are on the table. We have one piece, plus the eight ball, and it's my turn. When I make it, I debate on whether I want to ask this question or not.

"Make it good," he says with a small grin. "You're gonna miss the eight ball, and the next two questions will be mine."

I lick my lips. "Okay." I take a breath. "Are you in the closet?"

His brows draw together, and I await his, *what the fuck are you talking about* response, but instead he just continues to study me, his jaw clenching. The room is silent, and all we can hear is the wind howling on the other side of the cabin walls. Though it's probably freezing outside, the air in here is hot. Nearly suffocating. He keeps me waiting, and suddenly, I feel terrible for even asking.

"I'm sorry," I say. "You don't have to answer, just take your turn."

Ronan moves slowly, but he eventually gets in place, makes his last solid, then without asking me a question, sinks the eight ball. He drops his stick on the red felt, and I start thinking I really pissed him off.

He spins around, leans against the table and crosses his arms. "Are you attracted to me?"

The question catches me off guard, though I guess it shouldn't have. I just didn't expect him to ask me outright like this.

"Yeah," I answer simply.

He nods once, but doesn't look surprised. I guess I've made that pretty obvious.

"You didn't ask me the question I hoped you would," he says, looking off to the side.

"What question is that?"

"If I was attracted to your sister."

My heart drops to my stomach. He's trying to let me down easily. "I didn't ask, because I already know you do."

He nods, then finally looks into my eyes. "She's a beautiful girl, Renzo."

Fuck. My name coming out of his mouth is like honey—smooth and rich.

"But I'm not attracted to her."

I swallow thickly. "No?"

He shakes his head.

"Why are you hanging out with her then?"

He chews on his bottom lip briefly. "It's a long story, but the short version is she has a brother I find myself fascinated by."

The air in my lungs rushes out just as the power flickers then goes out.

"Shit."

Ronan

Chapter Eleven

BEFORE WE CAN EVEN DISCUSS what I just admitted, the power goes out and Renzo pulls his phone out of his pocket and turns on his flashlight. He walks out of the room, so I follow behind.

"I don't know where the damn circuit breaker is."

"It might just be the storm," I reply.

"Can you hold this?" he asks, handing me his phone. "Just aim it over here. I'll get the fireplace going."

Renzo grabs a giant box of long reach matches that rest on the mantel, then crouches down and reaches for the stack of newspapers nearby. He wads a few up and shoves them under the logs, before striking the match and lighting the paper on fire.

It doesn't take long before the fire grows, lighting up the room enough that we don't need our flashlights.

"I'm gonna call my mom real quick," he says, taking the phone from me, our fingers grazing.

"Okay."

I plop down onto the couch and stare into the fire. I just admitted to being fascinated by him, and eventually we're going to have to discuss that. What was I thinking? We just got here, and we have to be around each other for the next two weeks. I should've kept my mouth shut.

Renzo drops down next to me as I'm deep in my thoughts.

"Service was cutting in and out, but the gist of what's happening is that there's a bad blizzard happening outside, and Mom is keeping Vi and Dex over there with them."

"Oh." Thoughts I shouldn't be having run wild in my mind.

"Shit, I just realized Dex took my fucking car. I don't have all my shit."

"My car's outside, and I have plenty of clothes. They might be a little small on you, but..."

He turns and looks me up and down. "You're hardly small. You're almost my size, so it should be okay."

I try not to flush under his gaze, but thankfully it's dim in here, and I can blame reddened cheeks on the warmth of the fireplace.

"I should get the bag now, before it gets worse out there."

After I put my jacket on, I pull open the door and come to a stop. "Holy shit."

"What?" Renzo runs up behind me, his chest touching my back. "Oh fuck."

"It's worse than I thought."

Visibility is terrible. I can barely see my car, and it doesn't help that it's white, but I know I didn't park that far away. Half the tires are already covered in snow, so there's no way I'd be able to leave even if I wanted to.

I run down the steps of the porch, turning my head to the left to keep the freezing wind from whipping against my face. My feet sink into the fallen snow, making my trek a little harder.

When I find the door handle, I yank open the door and

grab both bags from the backseat. I try to run back, but the snow that comes up to my shins makes it difficult. When I hit the steps, my right foot slips and I nearly bust my ass.

Renzo chuckles, but runs out to grab a bag from me. We make it back inside and slam the door closed.

"Jesus Christ," I say, tossing the bag on the floor. "I don't know if those clothes were worth it."

"The alternative would've been nudity," he says, waggling his brows.

In order to keep from blushing, I turn around and take off my jacket to hang on one of the hooks near the door. I kick off my shoes and brush the snow from my pants.

"So, we're stuck here," I say.

Renzo's answering voice is farther away. "Yeah, and we have alcohol."

I spin around and see him in the kitchen, going through the cabinets. "What kind?"

He inspects the bottles in his hands. "Brandy and Gin." Looking at me, he pulls a face. "Must've been left by the last guests. Not what I'd choose, but hey, it's something."

"You planning on getting drunk?" I joke.

"I think we're gonna need something to get through this conversation we're about to have."

I slowly walk toward the kitchen, my hands in my pockets. "Ah."

"Yeah, don't think for a second that I forgot."

"Well," I grab a glass and push it toward him. "Fill me up."

He arches a brow, giving me a crooked grin.

~

"So," he says, dropping down into the corner of the couch, resting one long arm across the back while his other hand holds his Brandy mixed with Coke. "Why am I so fascinating?"

He smiles, and I'm grateful for the shots we took, plus this glass of Gin and orange juice I have. I didn't actually plan on telling him like this. Not now. Not out here with his family, but it felt right in the moment.

"Okay, let's start with something easier," he says. "Are you gay? Are you bi? Are you curious? What's goin' on?"

"Yeah. Easier," I snort. After taking a big gulp, my face contorts as I swallow it down. With a deep breath, I say, "I'm pretty sure I'm gay."

"Pretty sure?"

"I haven't been sexually attracted to women. I can admit when someone is attractive, but I don't want to sleep with women. I have no desire to do anything with them, honestly."

He nods. "But you do find men sexually attractive." It's a statement, not a question, but I answer anyway.

"Well, yeah," I reply, looking into my glass as my cheeks heat up.

He reaches out and lifts my chin with his finger. "Don't be embarrassed."

My tongue swipes my bottom lip as I gaze into his dark eyes, and he drops his hand. "I've never talked about this to anyone. My family..." I trail off, shaking my head. "They wouldn't understand."

"I've never had to deal with that," he tells me. "I was lucky. My family is amazing and never made me feel like I couldn't be myself. I told my sister first, and then I told my parents together at the dinner table. They just smiled and nodded and told me it was great. I can't imagine not having a support system, so I'm sorry you think they wouldn't understand."

I shrug. "They'll have to know eventually, right?"

He gives me a half smile. "I think you should tell them at some point. Give them a chance."

I take another sip. "Anyway, I haven't known anyone who was gay...until you."

His eyes bulge slightly. "Where the hell are you from that there's no gay people?"

"A very small, close-minded town. There were probably gay people there, but nobody who was out and proud about it. So, meeting you and then finding out you were gay, I was sort of in shock. When I saw you and that guy kissing..." I trail off, remembering all the thoughts and feelings that flooded my body.

"A little surprising, but also exciting?" he questions, his lips twitching.

I chuckle. "Yeah, something like that. And then at the pizza place, you just casually flirted with that guy, and then draped an arm around his shoulders before you walked out. I remember thinking, *it can be that easy? That simple?*"

"It wasn't always easy," he admits. "I went through the fear stage, too. How will those strangers react if they see me and another guy hold hands? Kiss? Hug? Do I ignore their dirty looks and loud whispers or do I confront them? Maybe I shouldn't do those things in public. But then I thought about it. Do straight people think about not kissing or hugging or holding hands with their significant others? Do they worry it will offend someone? No. So, why should I? I'm tired of people thinking being gay is taboo. It's not."

"So, do you still experience the stares and dirty looks?" I ask.

"Probably, but I've trained myself not to look. I don't need to know who's watching me and what they're thinking. I just worry about myself and ensure I'm doing something that makes me happy. Never allow yourself to be uncomfortable in order to make everyone around you comfortable."

I nod, rotating my wrist and watching the liquid slosh around in the glass. "I'll remember that."

"Good." He takes a drink. " So, is that why you're fascinated? You've finally seen something you've never seen before? A gay man? Gay guys kissing? A family that accepts their gay son and brother?"

"Yeah, it's new to me."

He nods his head, swallowing down the rest of his drink before placing it on the table next to him. "I see. So, tell me why you're stringing my sister along, then."

Chapter Twelve

I SWALLOW, my heart hammering in my chest as I study his face. I can't tell if he's angry or not.

"I'm not stringing her along," I state.

"No?" He cocks his head, an eyebrow arching slightly. "You've been to my house a handful of times, gone out with her, met my parents, and are currently on vacation with our family. She must think this is serious, or at least leading to something serious."

I set my glass down on the coffee table and shift to face him. "Look, let me explain."

"Please do."

"I like your sister. I really do. I think she's a great friend. She's funny and caring, and I hope to stay friends, but there's no way she can think we're serious. Now, before I say this next part, don't think I'm trying to talk down on her, but Violet is the center of attention wherever she goes. Every guy in a two mile radius is drawn to her, and she enjoys the attention. I've been around when she's talked and flirted with other guys. I don't think she's serious about me."

I stop talking when I see his jaw clench and unclench over

and over.

"Okay, maybe that came out wrong."

Renzo shakes his head. "I get it. Keep going."

"We've never done anything. We haven't even kissed. Well, okay, I kissed her on the cheek, but I'll admit where I was probably wrong." I take a deep breath. "I knew when she first approached me that there was a possibility that she was interested, and when she invited me to your house to eat and watch a movie, I started wondering if maybe she wanted more to happen, but I also thought maybe I should go with it. This is where my fear of being myself comes into play. But then I met you that night." His face softens a little, and I rub my palms across my knees and continue. "I wanted a chance to be able to see you again, so when she invited me to the party, I wanted to go. I wanted to see you."

Renzo scratches at the corner of his eye. "You know what I'm gonna say next, right?"

"That I used her?" I question. He nods. "I know. That wasn't right. Don't get me wrong, I do like hanging out with your sister. She's introduced me to some other people, and any time we've gone out, it's been as a group. We've always had a good time, but it's never been romantic. I started wondering if she was just okay with us being friends. She hasn't tried to make a move or anything."

He laughs. "She wouldn't. She's never had to."

"I almost didn't come on the trip. I didn't think it was a smart idea, but then you said you wanted me to come, and I couldn't say no."

Renzo shakes his head slowly. "You know this is beyond fucked up, right?"

I nod, rubbing my hands together as I drop my head and stare at the floor. "I'll talk to her as soon as I can."

"And tell her what?"

"That I want to be her friend, but that I'm gay. I don't

think she'll tell anyone if I ask her not to."

"She wouldn't do that, but that doesn't mean she won't be upset. Are you gonna mention anything about me?"

"Like what?" I ask.

"I don't know, like you kept coming around because you wanted to see me? She's gonna hate me when she finds that out."

"It's not your fault," I say.

He shakes his head. "I'm not gonna lie, I've had some terrible thoughts since you came around. I hated that you were interested in her. I hated that I couldn't flirt with you or have you. I was frustrated and jealous. And that's my sister. That's fucked up."

"She doesn't have to know any of that," I say, trying to clamp down my excitement over what he just admitted.

"She'll know if anything happens between us," he says, stealing the breath from my lungs.

"W-will something happen?"

He cuts his eyes to me. "Fuck, I hope so. I've had some filthy fantasies about you and that mouth of yours."

Warmth floods my chest and cheeks as my heart skips a beat. Subconsciously, I lick my lips at the mention of my mouth. "Oh."

"But we can't do anything now, which is the shittiest fucking thing, because we have this whole goddamn cabin to ourselves, and now I'm buzzed and horny, and I can't do shit about it. She's my sister, and even though it was fucked up of me to lust after you when I thought you were her boyfriend, I can't do anything to hurt her."

I nod, both respect and disappointment warring with each other in my brain.

"So, what do we do now?"

"I'm gonna go take a cold shower in the dark," I guess.

I laugh. "There's candles in the bedrooms."

Renzo stands up and grabs the matches. He stops next to me as he's about to leave the room. Our eyes stay connected for several seconds, and I can see the wheels turning in his head. He's fighting with himself.

"Fuck," he growls, stomping off.

I fall back into the cushion with a huff and press the palms of my hands into my eyes. I stay like that for nearly a minute before my phone vibrates with a text message.

I reach into my pocket and pull it out, reading the words across the screen.

> Hey, this is super shitty. Fucking blizzard has me staying with my parents!? Seriously? And Dex? Ugh. So sorry you have to be stuck with my brother. Are you okay?

> Hey, yeah, the storm is bad. I had to run out to the car to get my bags and nearly sunk into the snow and slipped trying to get back in. It's definitely good that you're staying there for the night.

> Ugh. My mom told me the weather is likely going to be bad for another day or so. If I'm stuck here another night, I might scream. What are y'all doing? Is he annoying you yet?

> Shit, I was thinking it would be fine tomorrow morning. I guess we'll see. We haven't done much, and no, he's not annoying me. Lol. He's pretty cool.

> I guess he's okay. Don't tell him I told you that though. Ha! He's also overly flirtatious and sexual, don't take it personally. I don't think he can control himself.

It's fine. How are you and Dex doing over there? Are your parents asleep yet?

Yeah, they went to bed a little bit ago. We're okay.

The power comes back on, and I hear Renzo say, "Thank fuck!" I chuckle, shaking my head, and get up to find a bedroom to stay in tonight.

After I grab my bags and throw them on the bed in the room I've claimed, I start unpacking and throw some stuff in the drawers of the dresser.

Remembering Renzo doesn't have his things, I grab a couple shirts, a pair of sweatpants, and some boxer-briefs, and make my way toward the room I think he went into earlier.

When I walk through the doorway, I mean to leave the clothes on the bed, but I hear him humming a song in the bathroom, so I stop to listen.

He walks by the partially open door, wearing only a towel around his hips. Renzo turns, giving me his back as he hangs his shirt over the shower rod. The muscles in his back flex, and my eyes travel from his wide shoulders down to his trim waist. Not an ounce of body fat is visible.

Renzo removes the towel from his hips, and brings it up to dry his hair, showing me his firm ass. I nearly gasp, my breath caught in my throat. I quickly rush out of the room before he notices me.

"Holy shit," I breathe once I'm back in my own room.

I've been pretty certain of my sexuality, though I never admitted it, but seeing a naked Renzo Hayes has completely solidified my gayness. The visual of his naked body remains in my mind, and my cock comes to life as I imagine touching the muscles along his back and squeezing that perfect ass.

I strip down to my underwear, ready to take my own

shower, and walk across the hall to the bathroom since I don't have an en suite. After I'm done, I wrap the towel around my waist and go back to my room to find Renzo lying on my bed.

His dark eyes slowly peruse my mostly naked body. "Jesus fuck," he breathes. "Are you trying to test my self-control?"

"I didn't really expect you to be in here."

"I wanted to say thanks for the clothes."

"No problem," I reply, making my way to the dresser and reaching for the lotion.

"Whatcha gonna do with that?" he asks lasciviously.

"Moisturize my body," I say with a laugh.

"Shame."

I start rubbing the lotion on my arms and then my chest and stomach, turning to find he's still watching me.

"Enjoying the show?"

"You have no idea," he answers, not looking me in the eye.

"I thought you said we can't do anything," I say, my voice getting a little breathy.

"We aren't doing anything."

"Well, here in a minute, I'm gonna have to drop the towel to lotion other parts of my body."

Renzo licks his lips, swallowing while getting to a seated position on the edge of the bed. "Okay."

I arch my brow. "You plan on sticking around?"

"I probably shouldn't."

He stands up and his growing erection is obvious in the pair of sweatpants I gave him, especially since they're probably a size too small.

Renzo runs his palm over it, making my pulse speed up.

"Yeah, I'm gonna go," he says before basically running out of the room.

Chapter Thirteen

ONCE I'M DRESSED in a T-shirt and a pair of sweats, I find Renzo in the kitchen making something to eat.

"Smells good," I say.

"Thank God my mom bought these frozen pizzas. It'll be ready soon. I figured I should use the oven now before the power goes out again."

"You think it will?"

"The wind hasn't let up, and based on the amount of snow still falling, I wouldn't be surprised."

"Violet said your mom mentioned it might be like this for another day or so."

"You talked to Vi?" he asks, spinning around to face me.

"Briefly. She complained about being stuck with your parents and Dex, and apologized for me having to be stuck with you."

He snorts. "Of course. I'm not that bad."

"She said you were overly flirtatious."

"Well, she's not wrong about that."

I hop onto the counter. "And here I thought I was special," I say with a smirk.

Renzo crosses the small space and steps between my legs, his hands resting next to my thighs. "Oh, you are. You're everything I've ever looked for and never found. Which is why not being able to touch you is killing me."

My Adam's apple bobs as I swallow, looking into his eyes. "What's everything you've looked for?"

His response comes without hesitation. "Eyes to get lost in. A perfect fucking mouth to sink my cock into," he says, carefully eyeing my lips. "An athletic body. A frame nearly as tall as mine." His gaze drops to my crotch before flickering back up and meeting my eyes. "There might be a couple other things that are yet unknown, but I have high hopes."

"Oh yeah?" I ask, already feeling hot and bothered, and he hasn't even touched me.

"Mm," he moans, leaning in, his body nearly touching mine. "I really hope you don't disappoint me, Ronan." My eyes close as his face travels up toward my neck. His breath dances across my ear, sending chills down my arm. "I think I might find out soon."

My cock twitches at his words. I open my eyes and find him just inches away. His lips catch my attention first, and I run away with thoughts about how they might feel against mine. Would he kiss me softly or aggressively? I wonder how that scruff on his face would feel against mine.

"You're making this really hard," I whisper.

"How hard?" he asks, grinning before biting down on his lip.

I reach into my sweats and grab the base of my dick while I stare into his eyes. "Really fucking hard."

His pupils dilate as the grin slips from his face, his jaw going slack. His gaze drops to my hand. "You're not wearing any underwear, are you?"

"I don't like to sleep in them," I say, stroking my length once.

"Jesus Christ." He backs up, leaning against the opposite counter. "Fuck, let me see it, Ronan."

"But—"

"I know what I said," he states, cutting me off. "We're still not doing anything. You're doing something to yourself, and I happen to be watching. There's nothing wrong with that, right?"

I smirk. "I think that's a slippery slope."

The timer goes off on the oven, and Renzo spins around to grab the oven mitts and take it out. While he's busy, I jump down and wash my hands.

"No," he groans. "Don't stop."

I chuckle. "You know we can't cross any lines. Even though I'm not with your sister, she should probably know before anything happens."

"Fuck. She probably won't even care," he grumbles. As soon as he's done slicing the pizza, his phone lights up on the counter. He picks it up and scans the screen. "Oh shit."

"What?"

"I think Violet knows."

"Knows what?" I ask, my brows pulling together.

"Fucking Dex," he says, unlocking his phone and quickly typing out a message. "Dex knows about my crush on you. I think he told Vi."

"What did she say?"

"Do you have a thing for Ronan?"

"That's it?"

"That's enough, right?"

My heart begins to pound in my chest. Her knowing Renzo likes me isn't the biggest deal, but this could potentially start a problem if she's mad about it.

"Maybe you should call her," I say.

"Yeah." He grabs a slice of pizza. "I'll be right back."

I touch his arm, stopping him. "Don't tell her about me. I'd like to be the one."

"Of course."

Once he's in his room, I start pacing the kitchen, wondering how to even go about saying it. Renzo is the first and only person I've ever told, and he made it easy by guessing. Maybe it's because he's gay, too. I don't know, but having to tell other people freaks me out. How will they react? What will they say?

I don't want the rest of this trip to be awkward. Eventually, we're all going to have to be together again, and what the hell will we tell their parents?

"Shit," I say, no longer concerned with food.

After what feels like an hour, I glance at the clock and see it's already after midnight. Renzo struts into the room with a sigh.

I spin around with wide eyes. "What happened?"

"She's gonna call you," he says simply, sitting on the couch.

"What the fuck? What did she say? What did you say? Was she mad?"

Before he can answer, my phone starts trilling.

Well, here goes nothing.

Chapter Fourteen

I **CLOSE** the door to the bedroom and bring the phone to my ear. "Hello?"

"Hey," Vi says.

"Hey."

Silence. So much awkward silence.

"So, um," she starts. A small giggle. "Me and Dex were drinking earlier, and he might've spilled some secrets."

"What secrets?" I ask.

"We were just talking and he mentioned how Zo is probably happy to be stuck with you. When I asked why, he said that Zo finds you attractive. Which, I get, because you are." She giggles again. "You know my brother's gay, right?"

"Uhh, yeah."

"Well, I guess he thinks you're cute. I mean, he admitted that to me just now."

"What all did he say?" I ask, needing to know, but also knowing that probably isn't the best question to ask right now.

"Not much, just that he's attracted to you and is jealous

that you're with me. I mean, even though we're not really together, you know?"

"Yeah."

She takes a breath. "Is there a reason why we haven't really done anything?"

"What do you mean?" It's a dumb question, because I know exactly what she means, but now that the time is here, I'm seeking more time to figure out what to say.

"I don't want to sound conceited or stuck up, but I've never really had to work too hard to get a guy to make a move on me. But you're harder to read. I thought you were just being a gentleman at first, which is appreciated, but after several weeks, we haven't done much more than hug and a couple cheek kisses. And to be honest, I loved having this new experience. I loved that it wasn't so easy, but now I'm wondering if maybe you're just not into me like that. Don't get me wrong, I'm not a slut. I'm not looking to sleep with you, because to be honest, I haven't...well, it doesn't matter, but I thought maybe we'd have done something by now."

Now's the time. Tell her. Just spit it out and say it.

"Violet, I do really like you."

She exhales before letting out a small laugh. "But?"

"I really didn't want to have this conversation over the phone," I tell her. "And probably should've had it several weeks back, but..." I take a deep breath and run a hand over my face. My knees bounce as I sit on the edge of the bed, then I shoot up and pace back and forth. "Well, I think... I mean, I know, but I haven't really told anyone."

"Ronan?" she says softly.

"Yeah?"

"It's okay."

My lungs deflate and I look up and see my reflection in the mirror. "I'm gay."

She's quiet for a little while, and I'm left to stare at myself and wait for her response. I knew in my heart that Renzo wasn't going to react badly, but now I'm admitting this to someone who isn't gay. To someone who thought they had a chance with me. Sweat forms under my arms as I continue to wait to see what she has to say.

"Wow, okay," she says, her voice low. "I didn't know." She laughs a little. "Well, that's obvious, right? I'm kind of embarrassed, but—"

"Don't be. I'm sorry," I say, cutting her off. "I don't want you to feel bad or anything. That wasn't my intention. Nobody knows. I'm trying to come to terms with it myself, and I thought I could pretend. Fake it till you make it, you know?" I blow out a breath, pacing again. "That sounds fucked up. I didn't want to hurt you or lead you on, I just thought...maybe it would work. I really like you. I love hanging out with you and your friends. You're funny and really nice, and I don't know. I'm rambling now. I feel like shit, honestly. I shouldn't have agreed to come on this trip. I'm sorry."

"Hey, it's okay. Look, you're right, this is probably a conversation we should have in person, but I'm not mad at you. I don't know what it's like to be in your shoes, but you know what? This probably worked out for the best. Renzo's there and he's the perfect person to talk to about this. His experience was different, but maybe he can share some stories and offer advice."

"Yeah, he's already told me a couple things."

"Oh. Did you already tell him?" she asks, her voice going high.

"Uh, well, he sort of asked. It's like he knew."

She laughs. "Is gaydar a thing?"

I chuckle, relief flowing through me. "I don't know. I'm still too new."

She cackles. "Well, I'm glad you have him there to talk to.

Just know that he's crushing on you, though, soo..." she trails off, and I wonder where this is going. "Wait. Do you like him, too?"

My heart threatens to beat out of my chest and fall to the floor. Another admission. Another truth. She took the first part of my news in stride, but will finding out that I've also been crushing on her brother make this weird? Will she hate me because I stuck around to keep seeing him? Fuck.

"Well, I don't know him too well, but I guess you can say I'm intrigued. I didn't know any gay people before, and Renzo appears to be unapologetically himself no matter where he is, and I was fascinated," I admit. "And okay, he's pretty okay looking."

Violet snorts. "Now I know you're lying."

I can't help the smile that takes over my lips. "Thanks for being cool with this."

She sighs. "I guess the saying is true. All the good ones are gay or taken."

I laugh. "Sorry, but I hope we can stay friends."

"Are you kidding? You're stuck with me. And if you and my brother start anything, good lord, you're gonna need me. But also, don't fuck with my brother's head. He deserves to be happy, and I'll ruin you if you hurt him."

"I'm kind of scared of you," I say with a laugh.

She giggles. "Good. Well, I'll let you go. Hopefully I'll see y'all tomorrow. Maybe the next day."

"Okay. Goodnight."

"Night."

After I end the call, I sit on the edge of my bed with a smile on my face. Only two people know I'm gay, but it already feels like a relief.

Chapter Fifteen

RENZO KNOCKS LIGHTLY, leaning his shoulder against the frame of the door. "How'd it go?"

"Good. Everything's fine. How was your convo with her?"

He takes a few steps inside, stopping at the dresser and perching his ass on it while crossing his arms. "I only admitted that I thought you were...decently attractive," he says, looking down at the grizzly bear figurine that's on the corner.

"Decently attractive?" I ask with a laugh.

His lips turn up as his head spins in my direction again. "Something like that. Fucking Dex got drunk and told her what I told him."

"And what did you tell him?" I ask, smiling.

"I might have said you were what my wet dreams were made out of."

Well, that wasn't the answer I was expecting. My smile fades away as my jaw drops. Renzo chuckles, and I say, "Are you fucking with me?"

"What? No. I really said that."

I shake my head. "Well."

"What did you tell my sister?" he asks, switching subjects.

"Well, uhh, she questioned why nothing had happened between us."

"Mhmm," he says, pushing away from the dresser.

"I told her I was gay."

Renzo takes a couple slow, methodical steps toward me, his face serious. "What else?"

"She felt embarrassed, and I apologized for leading her on." He stops a few feet away from me, his hands going into the pockets of the sweatpants that he makes look way too good. "She said it was good that we got stuck together because I could ask you questions."

His lips twitch before he sinks his teeth into the bottom one briefly. "And do you have any questions for me?"

My tongue swipes across my lip as I peer up at him. "Probably, but I can't really think right now."

Renzo smirks. "What else was said?"

"She asked if I had told you I was gay already, and I told her the truth—that you guessed."

He takes another step closer, and my heart rate ratchets up. "Is that all?"

"She asked if I liked you," I reply, my voice sounding breathier than I intended.

Another step. "And your answer was?"

"That you were pretty okay looking."

He laughs. "I see."

"She also threatened me."

His brow arches like he's surprised. "Hmm."

"Yeah," I breathe as he comes to a stop right in front of me.

I could touch him if I wanted to, and I do want to, but I'm also nervous.

"So, we're free to do whatever we want," he states, eyeing me like I'm his next meal.

"I-I guess."

He reaches out and runs his fingers through my hair, tilting my head back. "What do you want to do, Ronan?"

"I don't know," I answer honestly.

His hand moves around to cup my cheek, and then his thumb brushes across my bottom lip. While staring into his eyes, he pushes his thumb between my lips, and on instinct, I close my mouth and taste the soapy and saltiness of his skin.

Renzo moans, his eyes hooded and clouded with desire. He withdraws his thumb and grabs me by the throat, pulling me up.

"Let's start with a kiss," he says, his free hand finding my hip, while his other hand travels up to my jaw. "That okay?"

I nod, unable to find words as I study his handsome face.

He leans in slowly, and then his soft, warm lips touch mine. He's gentle and slow, not anything I'd imagine he'd be, but I can tell he's easing me into this—giving me a chance to pull away.

Renzo's tongue slides between my lips, tangling with mine, and the noise I make is a mix between a moan and desperate whimper. His hand moves to the back of my head, pulling me in closer as his other hand travels up my back, his fingertips pressing into my muscles.

His kiss sets me on fire, and the warmth in my stomach travels up to my chest, where my heart is currently beating out of control, and just as I think my knees might give out on me, he clutches me to his tall, strong frame, and I relish in how his body feels against mine. My arms wrap around him, and it's then that he releases his first moan, and it brings my cock to life in an instant.

"Fuck," he murmurs before kissing me again. Renzo brings both hands to the sides of my face, pulls back slightly to look me in the eye, then presses his lips against mine for a brief kiss. "I don't want to stop kissing you."

I crack a grin. "Then don't."

He growls, then devours my mouth again. Our lips and teeth clash together. I suck his tongue into my mouth, and then he bites my bottom lip.

"Christ," I moan.

He tugs my hair back, exposing my neck to him, and he leans in and licks a path up to my ear. "The things I want to do to you," he growls in my ear. "I want you bent over and fisting the sheets as I thrust in and out of your tight ass. I want your mouth on my cock, and I want your load on my tongue. Jesus Christ, I want it all."

I moan, a shiver running up my spine. "We definitely need to do something," I pant, my hands exploring the hard planes of his body. "My dick is harder than it's ever been."

Renzo steps back, his eyes traveling to my tented sweats. "Lay on the bed," he commands.

As I do what he says, he rips his shirt off in one quick movement, and I get to enjoy the sculpted god in front of me.

He crawls over me, straddling my legs, yanking on the hem of my shirt. "Off."

After removing my shirt, he runs his hands over my torso, and I close my eyes, enjoying the roughness of his hands on my body.

The bed shifts and I open my eyes and find him hovering over me. "I know you're new to this, so I'm gonna ask first. Do you want me to suck your dick? Or would you rather start slower?"

My heart skips a beat and my stomach clenches at the thought of my cock in his mouth. "No, not slower. That...that's fine."

He gives me a crooked grin before he starts planting kisses on my neck and chest. "I was hoping you'd say that."

My stomach quivers as his mouth explores my torso. My breaths come faster and deeper the lower he goes, and when he gets to the waistband of my sweats, his eyes flicker up and lock onto mine.

"Oh fuck," I murmur before shoving my hands in my hair and throwing my head back.

He tugs the elastic down, and I lift up to help the process. My dick springs free, slapping against my stomach. I glance down again and find him licking his lips in anticipation as he eyes my erection.

"Oh, Ronan," he moans. "Not a fucking disappointment at all. You're a goddamn dream come true."

He says nothing else before wrapping his long fingers around my cock and then taking me into his mouth.

"Ah shit," I exclaim.

His mouth is fucking magical. He takes me deep. So fucking deep. His hand continues to stroke me as his tongue twirls around my crown, and then he licks down my shaft and his tongue dances across my balls.

"Fuck, Renzo," I breathe, reaching down to grasp his head in my hands.

He groans and takes me deep in his throat again. The wet sounds of his slurping has my balls drawing up tight as his skilled hand continues to stroke me.

"Jesus Christ," I pant, watching my cock disappear into his mouth.

Renzo's eyes find mine, and he gives me a cocky wink before he finishes the job.

His hand moves fast and his cheeks hollow as he strokes and sucks like it's his goddamn job and he's looking for a raise.

"Shit. I'm gonna come," I warn him, dropping my hands to the covers and gripping them tightly as my muscles flex. Overwhelming pleasure travels through every nerve ending, and then I'm yelling into the room as my orgasm hits.

Renzo moans his pleasure when my cum lands on his

tongue, and he doesn't let up a bit until he's taken every last drop I have.

"Shit. Fuck. Oh my God."

He swipes his tongue over my crown before gently releasing my cock. "Mm. So fucking good."

Chapter Sixteen

"I CAN'T...I don't know..." I trail off, giving up on trying to make sense, and run my hand over my face and into my hair.

"I take it you enjoyed that," he says with a chuckle, coming up next to me.

My head flops to the side and I study his cocky grin and swollen lips. "Yeah, I did."

"So did I," he murmurs, coming in close and planting a kiss on the corner of my mouth.

"But you haven't finished," I say, pushing myself up to rest on my elbow.

Renzo's lips pull up on one side. "I didn't really have any expectations. You're a new, baby gay."

I roll my eyes, making a face at him. After a pause, I say, "What if I...want to?"

Turning to his side, he grazes his finger up and down my arm. "Do you?"

I chew on my lip before meeting his gaze. "I'd like to try."

He lies back, his hands locking behind his head as he grins at me. "I'll take whatever I can get."

Slowly, I get up and straddle his thighs, starting slow by

dropping down and kissing his lips. What I meant to be a quick kiss turns wild with passion as he grips my head in both hands and explores my mouth with his tongue. He arches his back, pushing his erection into my stomach.

I pull back and plant soft kisses on his collarbone, then down the middle of his chest, leading to his stomach.

My pulse jumps as I get lower. I chance a glance up at him as I'm sliding my fingers in the waistband of his sweats. His eyes are trained on me and they're full of desire. His teeth are digging into his bottom lip, waiting for what comes next.

With a quick tug, his erection pops free, slapping against his stomach. I swallow thickly as I work the pants the rest of the way down, then make my way back up.

I want to be good at this. I want him to be just as pleased as I was, but this is my first time, and the size of his dick is intimidating.

With a swipe of my tongue across my bottom lip, I reach out and grab the base of his cock, slowly moving my fist up and down, enjoying the feel of him in my hand.

"Shit," he breathes, briefly closing his eyes.

His skin is soft and warm, but his dick is harder than stone. After a couple minutes of stroking his length, I finally lower my head and open my mouth, taking the crown of his cock between my lips.

"Oh fuck," he groans.

He moves, but I don't look up at him. I keep my eyes closed as I slowly take him deeper, sliding him across my tongue and toward the back of my throat.

I come up, swirling my tongue around his shaft before sucking on his crown while I stroke him. He moans, and it's then that I open my eyes and study him.

He's watching me, his cheeks flushed. "Fuck, I knew my cock would look great between your lips."

My stomach clenches and my heart does a flip, then I take

him as deep as I can. My own dick comes back to life, and I reach between my legs to stroke it.

"Oh yes. You love having my cock in your mouth, don't you?"

"Mm," I moan around his erection.

Renzo runs his fingers through my hair, gripping the strands lightly, and then he moves his hips, fucking my mouth.

My hand quickens the strokes on my dick as he moves in and out of my mouth with fervor. His other hand joins the first, gripping my head as he does his best to keep from gagging me.

"Christ," he groans. "I'm gonna come soon. If you don't want to taste me, I'd suggest moving away."

I don't think about it, I just stay in place. If I'm gonna suck a dick, I might as well go all the way. Go big or go home, right? Plus, I want to know what he tastes like.

"Oh, God," he cries, pulling harder on my hair. "Oh shit."

Warm and thick, his cum lands on my tongue as he shatters below me, his body convulsing as he enjoys his climax. I swallow it down right away, continuing to stroke him slowly, tasting more of his release.

When his body relaxes, I slide my mouth down his shaft one last time.

"Jesus fuck. Come up here."

I do as he says, lying on my side next to him. "Good?"

He grabs my chin, staring into my eyes. "So fucking good."

My lips pull into a smile before he crashes his mouth onto mine. His hand finds my dick and he starts stroking.

"Oh, God," I cry.

"Renzo will do," he murmurs before sliding his tongue across mine. "I taste so good on your tongue."

Another moan is ripped from my throat. "Ah, shit. You're

so good," I say, fucking his hand.

"Oh, baby. You have no idea," he says, nuzzling into my neck before sucking a patch of flesh into his mouth.

"God," I cry, his hand moving faster.

"There's no god here," he whispers huskily. "Just me. Say my name when you come."

"Oh shit." My muscles tighten as pleasure blooms, bringing my orgasm to the surface.

"Come for me, Ronan. Come all over my hand and show me how much you love my touch."

"I'm so close," I pant, my eyes squeezed close.

"Look at me," he commands. I open my eyes and meet his gaze. "You came in my mouth, and you're about to come on my hand, just wait until you come in my ass."

I gasp, picturing it. "Oh," I whimper

"Yeah," he moans, covering my mouth with his just as I come.

"Renzo," I whimper, my body twitching, coming down from the release. His hand keeps moving, the slickness of my cum acting as a lubricant.

"Fuck, Ronan," he says. "It's so hot watching you fall apart under my touch."

My chest heaves as I suck in deep breaths, lying flat on my back with one arm over my eyes. "I can't believe I came twice."

"What can I say? I'm pretty skilled."

I let my arm fall behind my head as I look at him. "Cocky, too."

He moves fast, straddling my hips. "You like it, though." He brings his hand up, my cum coating his thumb and forefinger, and dripping down the back of his hand. "Here's the proof."

I grin, and he plants a quick kiss on my lips before getting off me and strutting to the door. I kind of hope we're snowed in for several more days, because I want Renzo all to myself.

Chapter Seventeen

WE DIDN'T PLAN or discuss sleeping arrangements, but after we both cleaned up, we went back to my room to lounge on the bed and ended up talking about random things before we both succumbed to our exhaustion and passed out.

When I wake up, I have a heavy arm draped over my waist, and a hard cock pressed into my ass. I can't help but smile as I try to remove Renzo's arm without waking him.

I make my way to the window and peek through the curtains to check on the weather. The fact that the sun isn't visible probably isn't good.

"Mm," Renzo groans behind me. "Bring that ass back to bed."

I chuckle, angling my head over my shoulder to see him stretching his arms out to the side. "The weather is still bad."

"Good," he replies, his voice deep and scratchy from sleep. "Means we have more time for just us."

"It's really coming down out there," I say, turning back to head to the bed. "I can barely see anything."

"Well, you know what's not coming down over here?" he questions, pointing to his visible erection, tenting the sheet.

I laugh. "Let me go to the bathroom first."

"First?" he questions with a raised brow. "Mm. Can't wait to find out what's second."

I roll my eyes and head across the hall to the bathroom. As I'm brushing my teeth, I hear Renzo's footsteps heading toward his room. He's probably doing the same thing as me.

Once I've washed my face and put on some deodorant, I make my way back to the room and go through the drawers looking for a pair of socks.

"What're you looking for, Prep?" Renzo's deep voice floats across the back of my neck as he traps me between his arms. His hands rest on the edge of the dresser, and his hard body pushes against mine.

"Prep?" I question, looking at him in the reflection of the mirror.

He smirks. "You look like a preppy runway model."

With a chuckle, I say, "I'm not sure how to take that."

"Oh, it's a good thing."

"Socks," I say, holding up a pair and answering his earlier question.

He dips his head, his mouth pressing kisses against my neck. We're both shirtless, wearing only our sweats, and I gotta admit, it's a sexy fucking sight seeing him behind me.

"I don't think you need those right now."

"Why's that?" I ask.

He kicks my feet apart, spreading my legs wide. "I wouldn't want you to slip."

I swallow as my heart threatens to leap into my throat. I watch him closely in the mirror, wondering what his plan is. "Oh."

A mischievous grin stretches across his face, and his right hand lands on my stomach, traveling up to my chest, and then gripping lightly on my throat. "I want to taste you."

Our eyes stay connected in the mirror and my tongue swipes across my lip. "O-okay."

Moving his hand to my jaw, he pulls my head back and plunges his tongue into my mouth, kissing me like it's the last time he'll do it, and man do I hope it's not, because this man's mouth is beyond talented.

Renzo pulls away quickly, forces my hands to the top of the dresser and says, "Hold on tight, and don't move."

Before I can question what's about to happen, he begins licking and kissing a path from the nape of my neck, down the middle of my back. I shiver, goosebumps forming across my arms as I watch him disappear behind me.

He tugs my sweats down until they pool at my ankles. I suck in a deep breath as soon as I feel the warmth and wetness of his tongue right above my ass.

"Oh, God."

"What did I tell you about that?" he says, kissing down one cheek while squeezing the other in his hand.

After teasing me with feather soft kisses, his hand pushes down on my back, forcing me into a bent over position, and then his tongue slides between my cheeks, tasting me in the most intimate area.

I tense up, but his hands grab my hips. "It's okay. Breathe. Relax."

I try to do as he says, but he's got his tongue in my ass, and part of me feels like that's wrong and gross, but as his tongue continues to swipe over my hole, it begins to feel good.

"Ohhh," I cry.

"Mmm."

His hands go back to my ass cheeks, spreading me apart so he can devour me. The tip of his tongue prods at the entrance, making me gasp before releasing a moan.

"Renzo, Jesus," I cry.

He stands up and leans over me. "You got lube in one of these drawers?"

"Second one on the left," I breathe.

He searches the drawer and comes up with a small bottle of lube, squirting some onto his hand.

With an arm around my chest, he pulls me up until I'm looking at myself in the mirror.

His slick fingers find their way back to my ass, sliding between the crevice. "You're so fucking sexy," he tells me, prodding at my opening. "You're gonna love this."

The tip of his finger breaches my hole, but he doesn't push in any further. Instead, he moves it in small circles, letting me get used to it while I gasp and moan.

"Oh fuck," I breathe.

"Ready for more?" he questions, kissing my shoulder.

I nod. "Yeah."

A fraction more pushes inside me, probably just to his first knuckle. "Fuck, you're so tight. Your ass is trying to pull me in. Attempt to relax. Don't clench."

I take a few deep breaths and he slides in a little deeper. "Holy shit," I pant, squeezing the edges of the dresser as my head drops down.

"You good?"

I raise my head and meet his eyes in the mirror. "Yeah. Keep going."

Renzo grins and pushes his finger all the way in. "Fuck, Preppy. I can't wait to slide my dick into this tight ass of yours."

He begins to move his finger around, easing out just slightly before moving back in. My body tingles with pleasure while also tensing with a little apprehension. I know it'll take time, but right now I can't imagine his massive dick being inside me.

Renzo moves, squeezing some lube between my cheeks, allowing his finger to move in and out with more ease.

"Oh fuck," I moan.

"Oh yeah," he growls, quickening his pace.

He reaches around with his free hand and finally touches my aching dick.

"Yes, please," I beg.

A low rumble in his chest lets me know he's turned on too. "You're already dripping for me," he says, smearing my pre-cum over my crown before starting to jack me off.

Something he does with his finger in my ass has me exclaiming. "Oh shit."

He continues to fuck me with his finger for another minute before carefully withdrawing and turning me around.

I gaze down at him. This sexy, filthy-mouthed god of a man is kneeling before me, ready to take my cock into his mouth. How the hell did I get this lucky?

The tip of Renzo's tongue teases my crown, circling it and licking a path down my shaft. His eyes continue to flicker up to my face, watching how I react to him. Honestly, the visual and the sensations are almost too much to handle. I'm not gonna last long.

His lips encircle my head, and ever so slowly he sucks me in deep, not stopping until his nose touches the coarse curls at the base of my dick.

"Jesus Christ," I breathe, my knees nearly giving out.

Renzo grips my thighs and worships my cock with his mouth. After several seconds, his right hand travels across my thigh, cupping my balls, and then a lone finger finds my hole. He pushes in slightly, but it's enough.

"Shit, Renzo, I..." I don't finish the statement. I don't need to. Jets of cum shoot out of my dick and into his mouth as he moans.

He continues to suck me as I have a full body shiver, my entire body affected by the orgasm.

With one hand on my shaft, he pulls back and lets his tongue dance across my head, making sure to lap up every drop.

As he gets to his feet, my legs tremble, so he grabs me by the waist and lifts me to sit on the dresser. His hands rest on either side of me as he leans in with a lopsided grin. "I'm gonna ruin you, Prep."

"What do you mean?"

He plants a kiss on my lips. It's brief. Chaste. I hate it and want more, so I cradle his face in my hands and pull him in, pushing my tongue into his mouth and tasting the remnants of my orgasm in his mouth.

When we separate, he grins. "I think it's already happened."

Chapter Eighteen

"I'M gonna go take care of this in the shower," he says, running a hand over his erection before stepping away from me. "You're driving me crazy here, Ro."

I drop down off the dresser and pull my sweats up. "I'm sorry," I start.

"Don't be," he says quickly, turning around and putting a hand on my cheek, his fingers resting at the back of my skull. "It's the best kind of crazy to be. I'm just dying to be deep inside you, but don't worry, I can be patient. We'll work our way to that eventually."

He winks and spins around, heading to his room. I follow behind. "You should let me watch," I offer, feeling nervous.

Without stopping, he looks over his shoulder, his lips pulled up on one side. "Oh yeah?"

Heat spreads across my chest and down into my stomach. "Maybe it'll help me learn what you like."

Once in the bathroom, he turns on the shower and then faces me. "You were pretty good last night, I don't think you need to study much."

I chew on my bottom lip, glancing down at the floor before meeting his eyes again. "Maybe I just want to watch."

He makes a noise that's a mix between a grunt and a growl. "See. Ruined. You're already turning into a sex fiend."

I chuckle. "We haven't had sex yet. There's no way I'm a fiend."

"Exactly. We've barely scratched the surface and yet you want to taste yourself on my tongue, and now watch me jack off in the shower." He tsks. "Who knew Mr. Preppy Pants would be into such things?"

"Shut up and get in the shower," I say, hopping onto the counter which gives me a perfect view.

"Mm. I like you bossy." He pushes his pants down, showing off his impressive cock. "But let's be honest, I like you every which way."

Renzo pushes the curtain back and steps inside. The water hits his chest first, then he turns around and gets his head wet. His biceps flex as he pushes his hair back, and I track the rivulets of water as they drip down his body. Water coats his flesh, traveling down the middle of his abs. His sex lines are well defined, that V shape bringing attention to his cock.

I lick my lips and let my eyes travel back up, finding his eyes on me.

He scrubs himself clean with a washcloth and soap, and I enjoy the flex of every muscle in his body. Who knew watching someone clean themselves would be such a turn on, but holy shit, he makes it look like a porno.

After what feels like ages, his hand slowly travels over his abdomen, gripping the base of his cock and then he gives it one languid stroke, squeezing at the tip before moving back again.

For nearly a minute, he jacks his dick while staring at me, but I can hardly keep eye contact, because I have much better things to watch.

He brings his other hand to his shaft and strokes his length with both, using a twist motion. His eyes close as his head drops back between his shoulders and he releases a seductive moan that gets me all riled up again.

He switches positions, resting a forearm on the wall in front of him, his head bent down as his hand moves quicker up and down his shaft.

"Christ," I whisper, feeling heat spread through my chest as blood rushes to my cock.

He angles his body toward me, allowing me a better view. His chest rises and falls with shallow breaths as he continues to pleasure himself with his eyes on me.

"You like what you see?" he asks, his voice breathy.

I nod, frozen in place, my eyes glued to the work his hand is doing.

Renzo hisses, then releases another moan that makes my dick twitch. "Ohhh."

I'm off the counter and rushing toward him. I don't care that I'm in sweats, I instantly step into the shower, drop to my knees, and take his cock into my mouth. It's only seconds before he comes on my tongue, but I'm glad I was able to taste him again, instead of watching him shoot off into the drain.

"Fuck, Ronan," he gasps, pulling me up. He slams his mouth against mine as water cascades over us, pulling away briefly to say, "You may just ruin me."

～

Once we're able to pull away from each other and put some clothes on, Renzo and I find ourselves in the kitchen, trying to make something to eat.

"So, what's this gonna be?" Renzo asks casually, his back to me as he cracks open an egg on the side of a pan.

"What do you mean?" I question, even though I'm pretty sure I know what he's alluding to.

With a spatula in hand, he angles to the side and glances at me. "You know. Your infatuation with me."

I roll my eyes and scoff. "Mm, I think it's a mutual thing."

He grins. "You're in the closet, I'm not. Do you think you're ready to be out to more than just me and Vi?"

I bite down on the inside of my bottom lip as I pull out a couple of bagels. "In theory, yes."

"In theory," he repeats, stirring the eggs in the pan. "What's up with your family?"

I blow out a breath. "Not open-minded at all. Being gay is a choice and an abomination."

He nods. "I see. That type."

"Right."

"Why aren't you visiting them for the holiday? Do they know about you?"

"I think my dad suspects. Toward the end of high school, I got a few questions about girlfriends, and my dad would look at me funny if I said I wasn't interested. They've never said anything outright, and neither have I. He's probably hoping I never tell them the truth, so they can live in their ignorance. They said they were going to visit my aunt and uncle for Christmas, and I didn't feel like going. I've never really felt like I belonged in my family."

Renzo eyes me before scraping the eggs onto a couple of plates. "You know me and Vi are adopted, right?"

Surprise blankets my face. "No, I had no idea."

"We don't really talk about it. Mom and Dad have been Mom and Dad since we were small, so they're our parents no matter what, but yeah. I don't know much about my biological parents except that they decided to give me up when I was two. Two," he repeats. "Have you seen a two-year-old? They're adorable and small. How can you not want that?" He shakes his head, grabbing the bagel and dropping it on his plate. "Anyway, for whatever reason, they decided after two years that they didn't want me, but my mom and dad did want me. They wanted me more than anything, and they brought me in and gave me an amazing life. I'm grateful to them for choosing me, and then later choosing Vi." He rests his hand on top of mine. "I say this because you don't have to be blood related to people to have a family. There will always be someone out there ready to accept and love you."

Chapter Nineteen

AFTER RENZO and I eat breakfast, he checks in with his mom and dad, and I get a text from Violet.

> Hey. Can you talk? Is Renzo around? Don't call me if he's around.

I eye Renzo as he walks around the kitchen, talking to his mom. I catch his attention and gesture to my phone, letting him know I'm gonna make a call, then I head into the room with the pool table and call Violet.

"Hey. He's not there, is he?" she asks right away.

"He's on the phone with your mom in the other room. What's wrong?"

Violet blows out a breath. "I think Dex tried to come on to me last night."

My brows pull together. "Okay, why do you say that? What did he do?"

"Well, we had been drinking a little bit, you know? And my parents were asleep, so we were just in the living room watching TV and talking and stuff. Nothing out of the norm. But then, he pushed his knee into mine, and when I looked at him, he just had this look. You know? Anyway, I let it go, but then when I was in the kitchen, he walked up behind me and brushed against my ass. I'm not stupid, I know he did it on purpose. When I narrowed my eyes at him, he just grinned and shrugged, then went about whatever the hell he was doing." She takes a deep breath. "Okay, but then, I was about to go to bed, and he walked with me and stopped in my doorway. He grabbed my hand and tugged me close to him and kissed me on the cheek."

"Okay," I reply.

"Ugh. That's not normal. We do not do that. I've known Dex for forever and he's never ever kissed me, but now he's grabbing my hand, touching my ass, giving me looks, and like saying things he's never said before. He's flirting. That's flirting, right? I mean, I know it is."

I chuckle. "Well, yeah, seems like it. Do you not like him?"

"No! I mean, yeah, but not like...I don't know. It's just weird. He likes me?" She says it like she can't believe it. "Anyway, on top of all that, Renzo will absolutely lose his shit over this. He can't know. Do not tell him. I'm serious."

"Okay, okay. I won't say anything. Have you talked to Dex this morning?"

"No. I spent an ungodly amount of time in the shower, pissing everyone off, then came straight to my room. They probably think I'm just being a moody teenager."

"I guess just play it by ear. Act like your usual self around him and see if he does the same. If he does anything else or says anything, then just call him on it. He has to know Renzo wouldn't like him being involved with you."

"Ugh. I know. All right, sorry to call and vent and ramble, but I can't tell anyone here. I'm so over this trip. The guy I came with ends up with my brother and now a guy who I've known forever is being flirty. It's a strange trip. Speaking of, did you and my brother do anything? I don't need details, but what's going on?"

I laugh, playing with the blinds so I can check the weather. "Don't make me feel bad, but yeah, I mean...some stuff has happened, but I don't know. Nobody knows about me, you know? So I don't know what's gonna happen once we leave here."

"I'm just messin' with you. I don't care that you like my brother. I mean, clearly I'm not your type, but if you had ditched me for another chick, we'd have problems." She laughs. "But I get it. It's still new for you. Don't feel rushed or anything. Hopefully everything ends up okay."

"Same for you over there. Think you'll be able to head over today? The weather still looks pretty bad."

"I know. Dad said the roads are terrible, and they're waiting for them to be cleared. We'll see."

"Okay. Well, text me later."

"I will."

After I slip the phone in my pocket, I turn around and find Renzo strutting through the doorway.

"Hey. Everything okay?" I ask.

"Yeah, they're fine. I guess Vi's having a fit over something. Mom said she's gonna take her food to her room because she refuses to come out. She's probably just being a moody teenager, mad that she's with her parents," he says with a chuckle.

I crack a grin, loving that she knew exactly what they'd say about her. "I see."

"The wind hasn't died down and the roads are completely covered. Probably looking like we won't see them until tomorrow."

He comes to a stop right in front of me, and his fingers find my belt loops right before he tugs me into him. "So, we have all day to ourselves."

"What're we going to do?" I ask, my eyes drifting to his mouth.

Those perfect fucking lips pull up on each end and mischief twinkles in his eyes. "I might be able to think of some things."

"Oh yeah? Will it take all day?"

"I could make sure it does. You're still so new," he says, his hands moving around my hips and cupping my ass. "But there's so much we can do before I find my way deep inside you."

My eyes close as I drop my head back and inhale. My stomach tightens at his words, and my cock seems to like them, too, because it twitches behind my jeans. "I'm always ready to learn new things," I say once I've composed myself.

"Maybe I'll let you find your way deep inside me," he whispers, kissing a patch of skin behind my ear.

My breath catches and my hands explore the muscles of his back. "Oh."

"It's not too different from fucking a chick. Just tighter and better."

His hand comes around and rubs over my cock. "I...uhh..."

Quickly, he pulls back, his brows furrowed. "Wait. Are you a virgin? Like, you've never fucked around with a girl either?"

"I told you I wasn't sexually attracted to them."

"Yeah, same, but even I tried it. Definitely something I'm not in a rush to do again, but yeah, I did it."

"I've never even wanted to try," I say with a shrug.

"Wow," he breathes, running a hand through his hair. "This will be fun."

A sigh of relief leaves me as soon as I see that crooked, cocky grin of his. "I hope so."

"I didn't bring condoms, so we'll worry about that when we're back home. For now," he says, grabbing my waist and yanking me into him, "I have plenty of other things we can do."

I tentatively run my hand up his torso, landing on his chest. Even though we've been naked together and sucked each other off, I still feel nervous around him. I hope I'm not coming off as inexperienced as I am, but I'm afraid I'll get something wrong and mess up our experience.

Like he knows what I'm thinking, his lips twitch as he fights off a grin, then he reaches up and grabs my hand, kissing my knuckles before pushing it down to grab his cock.

"Let's get started."

Chapter Twenty

IN RENZO'S BED, he strips me naked before removing his own shirt and straddling my thighs. Leaning over me, he plants hungry kisses across my neck and collarbone, grinding his erection against mine as his mouth explores my chest. His tongue flickers over my nipple before he captures the hardened tip between his teeth, eliciting a hiss from me.

"Ahh."

He plants a soft kiss on the sensitive flesh to makeup for the pain, then keeps moving lower. His body slides down my legs as his tongue licks the underside of my crown, traveling down to my balls.

"Oh, God," I breathe, tightening my grip on the covers.

Renzo works his magic on my cock, licking and sucking me into his mouth, bringing me an intense amount of pleasure I didn't know possible from just a blowjob.

He seems to know I'm getting close, because he eases off, removes his pants, then straddles my thighs again.

Reaching over, he grabs the bottle of lube he placed on the bed, squirts some into his palm, and then begins to stroke himself.

"We're gonna come together this time," he says.

He grips our cocks together in his lubed up hand and begins stroking.

"Oh shit," I say on a breath, looking down at where we connect.

His large hand moves up and down, and the visual makes the experience so much better. Our dicks are engorged, rubbing against each other while his hand adds more friction.

"Feels so good," I say around a moan.

"You do it," he pants. "Put both hands around us."

I bring my hands up, my thumbs touching my cock while my fingers rest on his. "Like this?"

"Tighter," he says, starting to thrust.

"Oh shit," I exclaim.

Renzo moves quicker, his cock rubbing against mine and in the space between my hands. It's better than any hand job I've given myself. Having his hot and hard erection pressed against mine while also being able to feel the veins of his cock sends heat through my core.

His low and deep grunts and moans of pleasure are music to my ears, causing my balls to tighten up as I watch him move on top of me.

"Renzo," I breathe.

"Yeah, babe," he says with a grunt.

"Oh God, Renzo."

"Yeah," he says with a pant. "I'm close."

I tighten my grip, and a few seconds later, cum shoots out of my cock, landing on my stomach. "Fuck!"

Renzo looks down, and then his body flexes and his back hunches, his own orgasm hitting him hard. He takes his cock into his hand and ejaculates onto mine. The thick, white liquid lands on my crown before dripping onto my stomach.

"Oh my God," I moan, turned on at the sight. "Holy shit."

He grunts, squeezing his cock as he continues to drip onto me. I stroke my erection, using his cum as lubricant, and my body convulses with a tremor.

Renzo collapses next to me, his breathing just as heavy, if not heavier than mine. "Fuck, Ronan. Fuck, fuck, fuck."

Blissed out, I just blow out a long breath. "Yeah."

Renzo

Chapter Twenty-One

I WASN'T LOOKING FORWARD to coming on this trip, but now I couldn't imagine not being here. The blizzard really helped me out, and I'm not one to believe in miracles, but I'm pretty sure Mother Nature was on my side here. Had Ronan and I not been stuck here together, who's to say I'd have had the opportunity to even question his sexuality. Typically, it's not something I do, and honestly, it's pretty rude, but I was picking up on certain vibes and I couldn't take it any longer.

Luckily for me, not only is he gay, but he's just as into me as I'm into him.

I'm drying my hair with a towel as another one hangs around my hips when Ronan walks in. His eyes peruse my body for a few seconds before they meet my gaze.

"Fuck, you'd think we haven't been coming all over the place the last twenty-four hours," he says, palming his cock through his pants.

I grin and crook a finger at him. He smiles, coming toward me. I pull him in for a kiss, my hand wrapped around the back of his head.

"Better get our fill of these moments before the rest of the gang join us tomorrow."

"I hate to sound like an ass, but what's the chances of having another blizzard?" he questions.

I chuckle. "Sadly, it seems to be clearing up."

"When will we be able to do anything?" he asks, a tinge of pink coloring his cheeks.

Fuck, I love how innocent he is.

"We can sneak behind their backs," I say, moving my hand under his shirt and around to his ass. "A quick kiss in the hall, or a grope under the table."

His tongue snakes across his bottom lip. "And what about when I want to try more?"

"Mm. Don't tease me, Preppy."

He grins. "Sorry."

"We'll figure it out. Don't worry."

"I'm gonna go find something for us to eat," he says, turning away from me. "Put some clothes on so I can focus."

I laugh. "No promises."

Once I'm dry, I do put on another pair of his sweats, but choose to stay shirtless just for the fun of it. The heater is blasting, so it's not like it's cold in here.

We spent all day fucking around, unable to keep our hands and mouths to ourselves. At one point, when the wind had died down, we went outside to walk around, then came back in to warm up and ended up sucking each other off again.

I'm already addicted to him, and it's gonna be hard as hell to go back home and not be able to touch and kiss him whenever we're together. Everyone knows I'm flirtatious and never without a guy for too long. Now I'm gonna have to figure out how to play this off.

∼

"Get up, get up, get up!" Violet's voice hits my ears, and confusion mars my face before she shakes me again. "Mom and Dad are here, idiot. Get the fuck up!"

I jolt up, suddenly aware of what's going on. "What time is it?"

"Get up, Ronan," she whisper yells. "It's eight."

I grab his hip and shake him. "Hey, we gotta get up."

His hair is all over the place when he jolts forward. "What?" He spots Violet. "Oh. Oh!" He's out of the bed, reaching for his shirt and yanking it over his head with lightning speed.

"I'll go keep them distracted," Vi says, grinning as she watches us freak out. "By the way, Zo, you fucking owe me."

"For what?"

"I'm gonna go to the bathroom," Ronan says, rushing between us.

"For being the best sister in the whole world. For being cool as shit and letting my boyfriend hook up with my brother."

I scrunch my face up. "Ew, don't ever word it like that again. He was not your boyfriend, and you know that."

"Yeah, well, you know. I'm still the best, so you owe me for not being dramatic about it."

After I pull on a shirt, I smile and squeeze her cheeks between my hands and kiss her forehead. "You are the best, and I love you."

She pushes my hands off of her. "Yeah, yeah. I love you, too. Honestly, I'm glad he's gay. I was starting to worry I had lost my touch."

I shake my head. "Anyway. Go distract Dex. I don't want him looking for me. I have to brush my teeth and get Ronan to his room without him seeing."

"Ugh. Fine."

~

Twenty minutes later, we're all in the kitchen as Mom makes breakfast.

"Sorry for barging in so early," she says. "I didn't want to risk waiting and have the weather take a turn. Were you two up late?"

Ronan fidgets slightly and I grin remembering it was damn near two o'clock when we passed out after I swallowed his load and shot mine all over his stomach. "Sort of. Just eating junk and playing pool."

"Oh, that's nice," Mom says, focusing on cooking. "Grab the plates, dear."

I place them next to the stove and then hop onto the counter. Mom gives me a disapproving look but doesn't say anything.

"So, what did y'all do while you were trapped together?"

"Well, I got a lot of reading in, and I made a couple pies."

"Vi, what about you?" I ask. "Did you stay locked in your room the whole time?"

She gives me a fake smile before flipping me off behind our parents backs. "No. Not the whole time. We watched TV and talked and, yeah, I don't know. I just slept or played on my phone."

"Fun."

"Well, we can't all be so lucky to be trapped in a blizzard *without* our parents, now can we?"

"Hey, we're not that bad," Dad quips from behind a newspaper as he sits at the dining room table.

"Well, at least you had Dex," I say, cutting my eyes to my best friend.

Violet scoffs and Dex shifts his stance, glancing up from his phone.

"What did I do?"

Vi narrows her eyes at him, opens her mouth to say something, then changes her mind. "Never mind. Anyway, I just would have rather been here."

Mom chuckles. "Well, of course you would have, dear. Your boyfriend was here, and while I really like Ronan, I'm glad it turned out the way it did." Mom turns and winks at Vi.

"Oh right, yes. My boyfriend." Ronan's eyes bounce between mine and Vi's. "Because we could've been handsy with each other if we were here alone."

"Violet," Dad warns, peeking over the paper.

"That's what you're saying though, right? That I wouldn't be able to control myself? You never worry about Zo doing stuff. He's always hooking up with people."

"Hey!" I exclaim, throwing my hands up. "Why am I being thrown under the bus?"

"Of course we worry about Renzo, but he's an adult now and can take care of himself. You're only seventeen," Mom says softly.

"I'll be eighteen soon, and I'm very capable of taking care of myself."

"We know," Mom says, placating her.

The room settles into an awkward silence.

"Oh, Renzo, guess who I ran into at the grocery store the other day," Mom says, changing the subject.

"Who?"

"Kris."

"Oh. Cool."

I never know how to talk about my ex-boyfriend, but I really don't want to talk about him in front of my...whatever Ronan is to me now. Fuck buddy? That seems wrong. Boyfriend? Nah.

"Yes, and he asked about you. He was always such a nice young man. He said he's doing a nursing program now."

"That's good, Mom."

"Anyway, he said he might give you a call sometime. Maybe you two can work out whatever happened."

I shake my head and hop down from the counter. "Yeah, I don't know."

"With all due respect," Dex cuts in, "Kris was sort of a douche."

"What?" Mom exclaims, her eyebrows shooting up toward her hairline.

"It's okay," I tell Dex. He knows what happened between us, so I know where this is coming from.

He shrugs. "Just saying."

Mom looks me over, waiting for some extra information, but I just put my hands on her shoulders and kiss the top of her head. "It's okay, Mom. I'll find someone eventually."

"Well, don't find anyone in the closet. You know how that turned out before."

My eyes instantly meet Ronan's before finding Violet's pity-filled gaze.

"There's plenty of out guys at school, "Dex says, walking to the table and pulling out a chair next to Violet.

"Ronan's gonna sit there," she says, putting her hand on the seat and then gesturing for Ronan to sit down.

"Oh right," Dex says, moving to another chair. "Anyway, there's a few gay guys in some of my classes, and I know one of them has it bad for Zo. Want me to hook you up?" he asks with a grin.

"No thanks."

"Oh, right! Didn't you just..." he shifts his eyes between my parents, "hang out with Jayden's friend? Brantley? Barrett?"

"Bryant," I correct him. "And yeah, that's not anything."

"How do you even find closeted guys to date? I mean, if they're in the closet, how do you know?"

"You know," I say, doing my best to not look right at Ronan. "Sometimes you just know."

"Food's done!" Mom chirps, ending all conversation.

For the duration of the meal, Ronan never looks at me, and based on his tense demeanor, I'd say something definitely got to him.

Could be the talk of my ex, the talk of the guy I just had a quick hookup with, or my mom saying not to date closeted guys. Regardless of what it is, I definitely need to find time to talk to him soon.

Chapter Twenty-Two

AFTER WE EAT, everyone bundles up and heads out to get to the dunes, where we spend a good forty minutes or so sledding.

After that, we don our snowshoes and find a trail that's usually a seven mile car loop, but since traffic is closed off in the winer, we get to walk the same trail and see the scenic overlooks.

"I hope we're not planning on doing the whole seven and a half miles," Vi complains. "That's way too long."

"You can do as much as you want, sweetie," Dad says, moving ahead with Mom. "Just make sure if you turn back, be with one of the boys."

Me and Dex walk a little ahead of Vi and Ronan, and a ball of jealousy and annoyance grows in my stomach. I hate that I can't use this time to be with him, walk with him, laugh with him. Dex doesn't know about Ronan, so I can't say anything to out him, and Dex and my parents still believe Ronan and Vi are dating, so it makes sense for them to hang out, but I wish we could be together.

This is why being with closeted people is hard. I don't like to hide and sneak and keep things to myself, and yes, while sometimes sneaking around can be fun and exciting, I enjoy being out in public and being able to hold my guy's hand, or just do regular couple stuff. However, I can also understand where he is in his journey, but like Mom brought up before, I've been down this road before, and I didn't like it.

"Okay, scenic overlook! Let's take selfies!" Violet squeals.

She hurries over and snaps shots of herself first, and when the rest of us get close, she has us all squeeze together while she extends her arm and takes a picture.

"Ugh, Renzo!" she scolds.

"What?"

She shows me her phone, at an angle only I can see, and points at my face. I'm looking at Ronan like I want to lick him up and down. Which is true, but I can see the problem.

"Well, do a countdown. I wasn't ready."

She does the slowest, most obnoxious countdown, and takes another photo. I use this time to wrap my gloved pinky around his and tug on it. He quickly looks my way before playing it off.

"Okay, Dex, take one of me and Zo. Then me and Ronan."

She shoves the phone in his hand and pulls me to her side. We take our photos before she takes photos with Ronan.

"Okay, now you three."

"Why?" Dex asks.

"Just do it!"

I stand in the middle and rub my hand down Ronan's back and rest it on his ass. Too bad we're so bundled up, but I'll take what I can get.

I walk over to Vi and peek over her shoulder. "I may want a couple of those," I whisper.

"I know. Don't worry."

"Have I told you you're the best?"

"Not for like four hours, which is clearly too long."

"Clearly."

She angles her head and grins at me. "I could maybe hang back with Dex if you want some time. I mean, I don't know what the hell we're gonna do, and also, he's been weird and annoying, but I'll take one for the team."

I smile at her. "I'm not sure what a good excuse would be to get you alone with Dex that allows us to go off on our own."

She lifts a shoulder. "I'll figure something out."

"You're the best."

"I know."

Ronan continues to wander around, checking out the scenery, and Dex yanks off his gloves to use his phone. I head in his direction, already prepared to distract him. I definitely owe her something. Kind of afraid of what it'll be when it's time to pay up, but she'll make it a good one for sure.

I approach Ronan from behind. "Hey."

He spins and starts to grin before looking toward Dex and Vi to see if they're watching. "Hey."

"You okay? Seem a little off since breakfast."

He averts his gaze to the ground, kicking at the snow. "Just thinking."

"Yeah? Well, why don't you tell me what you're thinking about?"

"What about them?"

I lift my head and spot Vi gesturing wildly with her hands. "Hey! You good?"

She meets my gaze and waves me off. "You guys go ahead, I'm gonna talk to Dex for a few. We'll meet up."

I make a show of looking confused so Dex doesn't think it's weird, furrowing my brow and throwing my arms up. "Okay. Take care of my sister, Dex," I say, pointing a finger at him.

He raises his hand, then I smile at Ronan. "All taken care of. Let's go."

We walk nearly twenty feet down the trail before he says anything. "So, you've been with a *few* people." He emphasizes *few*, letting me know he's aware it's much more than that.

I snort. "Are you trying to call me a whore?"

"No, but you're experienced."

I nudge his arm, smirking. "More than you."

"And you've been with someone who was in the closet? What happened there? Your mom didn't seem too fond of that situation."

I sigh. "Yeah, well, it wasn't the best situation to be in. We were together for, I don't know, six months. Anyway, I'm an outgoing kind of guy. I like to be out and about, you know? On top of that, I don't really like to hide who I am. If I'm with someone, I want to touch them, kiss them, flirt with them. Anyway, I did it for a while, and he said he was going to come out, but he never did and it really put a damper on our relationship. He could only come to my place, and if we were at the same party, he'd stay far away from me because he was so worried people would assume he was gay if he was talking to me too long. It started to feel like he was ashamed, and I didn't like the way it made me feel about myself."

Ronan nods. "I can understand that. And Kris? He was a serious boyfriend?"

I take another deep breath and let my eyes roam over the tops of the frozen trees. "Yeah. The only serious one. I thought he was *the* one."

He looks at me. "You loved him?"

I nod. "I did. I told him so. He didn't feel the same way."

"Oh. I'm sorry."

I wave it off. "It's kind of weird to talk about with you, to be honest," I say with a chuckle.

"Sorry."

We round a curve and walk toward the frozen lake, completely out of sight from Dex and Vi. "It's okay. The breakup is fairly recent, if I'm being honest, and I didn't really get closure on it."

"What do you mean?"

"Well, after the embarrassing and awkward minute after I told him I loved him, and he said nothing, he stood up quickly, gathered his stuff and said he had to go. Sort of the typical movie situation where a girl tells a guy she loves him and he freaks out because he's not ready for commitment. Except, we had been together for almost a year. We were committed and happy. Later the next day, he texted me and said we should take a break."

"A break?"

"Don't worry," I say with a smirk. "It's not like the Ross and Rachel fiasco. We're one-hundred percent broken up. I haven't heard from him since."

"According to your mom he's gonna reach out to you soon."

"I wouldn't read into that. He was probably just being polite."

I watch him out of the corner of my eye as he chews on his bottom lip. When we get to the edge of the lake, he speaks up.

"I guess I'm just a little confused and afraid."

"Explain," I say softly, grabbing his hand.

"I know I like you and want to keep doing whatever it is we're doing." Though his cheeks are already red from the cold, I swear they get redder as he blushes. "But now I kind of feel bad about putting you in a situation you've already been in and didn't like. However, I'm still afraid of coming out. And honestly, I'm concerned if I don't live up to what you need, you may go back to Kris or Bryant or the guy you were kissing at the party, or anybody. You could have anybody."

"Are you wanting to call it quits?" I ask.

He looks into my eyes. "No."

"Then let's take it one day at a time."

Ronan hesitates for a few seconds before his lips turn up on one side. "Okay."

I glance around, making sure Vi and Dex are nowhere to be found, and then I press my lips to his. He tenses up at first and then melts into me, kissing me back.

"Too bad we're out here in the cold because I really want your dick in my mouth right now."

He bites his lip, a smile growing. "Maybe tonight?"

I arch a brow. "Risking it, huh? I'm down."

Chapter Twenty-Three

IT'S NEARLY eight o'clock when we finish the dinner mom prepared for all of us—beef and Guinness stew.

"Hot chocolate, anyone?" Mom asks from the kitchen as the rest of us sit in the living room around the fire.

"Can you put whiskey in mine?" Dad asks. "You know what, just whiskey and a handful of marshmallows to snack on."

"Theodore!" she chides. "If you think I'm driving us home on these roads, you've officially lost your mind. You can have hot chocolate or nothing."

Dad chuckles low, glancing at us with a grin like he gets a kick out of riling her up. Which he does. "Okay. Sorry, Dear."

"Mhmm," Mom murmurs, already bringing over mugs to pass to each of us. "You're never too old for hot chocolate."

"Thanks, Mom," I say.

"Yes, thank you," Ronan says, taking a mug.

"Of course. I'll be back with the rest."

After everyone finishes their drinks, we talk about our plans for the next day, and then Mom and Dad prepare to leave.

"Okay, so we're trusting you all to behave yourselves," Mom says, dropping her chin to her chest like she's looking over the top of glasses she's not wearing. "Lorenzo, you're the oldest and I expect you'll keep things in order."

Violet barks out a laugh, but Mom shuts her up with a quick glance. "And no funny business." Her eyes bounce between Vi and Ronan, and it takes a lot to keep from laughing as well.

"Don't worry, Mom. I'll sleep between them if I need to."

She purses her lips at me and softly smacks my arm.

"Yeah, why don't they just room together since I'm not to be trusted," Vi quips.

I look over my shoulder with a grin.

"Don't be silly. There's enough rooms for each of you to have your own. Just be smart."

She leans in and kisses me on the cheek, and Dad pats me on the shoulder and gives me a firm nod. "I know you won't let anything happen."

"Nothing will happen between those two on my watch."

Vi scoffs and Ronan tries to slink in the background, probably uncomfortable.

"Night, Mr. and Mrs. H," Dex says with a wave.

"Night, Dex. You be good, too."

"Always."

Mom makes a face. "Right."

As soon as the door closes behind them, Violet yells, "Party!"

"Violet!" Dad threatens on the other side.

"Just kidding!"

"Why do you like pushing their buttons?" I ask.

She shrugs. "So, what're we doing now?"

"I don't know. We can play pool, watch TV, or go to sleep. There's not many options."

"Lame. Fine, let's play pool first," she says, pulling Ronan by the wrist.

"Your sister is a handful," Dex says.

"I know. Was she mad at you earlier?"

"Yeah, I guess. She didn't like something I said. I don't know." He shrugs it off and heads in the direction of the pool room.

"Teams?" I ask, grabbing a stick.

"Sure," Vi answers.

"I'll be on Ronan's team," Dex offers.

I laugh. "You just don't want to lose to him again."

Violet skips over to me with a grin. "We got this," she says, hitting her elbow against mine.

Dex shoots a worried look to Ronan. "I hope that wasn't beginner's luck earlier."

We let Ronan break, and after one solid ball drops into a pocket, Dex tries for another and misses. Violet steps up to the table and sinks her first shot. I make the next, and she gets another.

"What the fuck?" Dex exclaims. "Fucking pool sharks or what?"

Me and Vi laugh as I walk around the table, looking for my next shot. "We have a pool table in our basement. When Mom and Dad worked all the time, we spent all our free time down there. Plus, Dad had a friend who was this professional pool player and he taught us some things."

"I've never seen you play pool before," Dex says, looking at Violet. "And you clearly have been taking it easy on everyone."

I smirk and give him a one shoulder shrug.

"I don't play a whole lot anymore," Vi answers.

Dex walks toward her. "You should hit up the bars and take money from people. They wouldn't expect you to go in and whoop ass."

Vi cocks her hip. "Why? Because I'm a woman? Because women can't be good at pool?"

"I- I was just saying."

"Yeah, well, I'm underage. I can't go to bars."

"We play pool at Jay's frat house sometimes. You could hustle money from frat guys."

"Maybe. When's the next party?"

I tune them out as Ronan steps up to the table, right in my sightline. He runs his hand down the front of his pants, bringing my attention to where his cock rests behind his sweats.

My eyes flicker up. "Need something?"

He grins. "Maybe."

"I know you're trying to distract me."

I reposition myself, my ass sticking out as my stomach hovers over the edge of the table. My fingers are perched on the felt with the stick sliding between them, ready to take my shot.

"If I were to slide into you, would you be in this position?" he asks softly, right as I send the stick into the white ball.

Instead of hitting the ball straight-on, I skid it across the felt and fuck up the whole shot. The ball doesn't go as far as I need it to.

I stand up and find Ronan smirking at me.

"I'll remember that."

"Oh, I hope so."

When Ronan starts to take aim, Vi looks over. "You missed?"

"I had a spasm," I lie. "Don't worry about it."

Ronan makes his shot, and Dex makes his, except he scratches, so Vi takes her turn and sinks it in. They don't get a chance to make any more shots, because me and Vi end up finishing the game on our turn.

"Cheaters," Dex mumbles.

"Hater," Vi says with a cutesy grin.

Dex doesn't want to play anymore after that, so Ronan and I go a round and then he and Vi play against each other. It's almost ten, and while it's still technically early, I can't stop thinking about getting some alone time with Ronan.

"I think I might head to bed soon. I didn't get nearly enough sleep last night."

"What? Dude, it's only ten o'clock! Don't be lame," Dex says.

"I'm sorry, man. I'm beat. Night, y'all."

I disappear through the doorway and down the hall, hoping like hell that Ronan decides to come to my room.

Ronan

Chapter Twenty-Four

AS SOON AS Renzo leaves the room, I feel his absence deep in my bones. It's weird, because I haven't known him very long, but these last couple of days brought us closer than I thought possible. We've had hours and hours to talk, get to know each other, flirt, and mess around. Thanks to the storm, we've been inseparable for over forty-eight hours, and now that he's not around, everything feels different.

He's already allowed me to be my most authentic self around him, and though my nerves are out of control when he's nearby, I haven't felt more comfortable around anyone else. I know it's because he knows about me, and more than that, he's not judging me in the least.

With Violet and Dex here, I feel a tiny wall being built back up as I slip back into the comfort of my closet. Even though Vi is aware of my sexuality and the situation with her brother, because Dex is around I feel like we're both putting on a front. I mean, we are. We have to pretend we're together. I have to pretend I don't want to chase after Renzo.

"So, what's up with you, Ronan?" Dex asks with a lift of his chin.

"What do you mean?"

"Well, I don't know much about you, yet you're here on a trip with the Hayes family."

"Are you a part of the Hayes family?" I counter.

He shifts, his jaw clenching as Vi giggles. "No, but I've been best friends with Zo since we were six. I'm basically family."

My eyes shift between him and Vi. "Interesting. Well, I don't know what to tell you, Dex. I was invited, so I came."

"Why are you being so weird?" Vi asks Dex, making her way to my side, grabbing my bicep to play up our roles. "Ronan's a good guy."

"I'm not being weird, I'm just trying to get to know the guy." He looks me up and down. "Since apparently he'll be around quite a bit."

"Come on, let's go get something to eat," Vi says, changing the subject.

"Actually, I'm probably gonna crash," I tell her. "I'll see you tomorrow?"

She nods, glancing over her shoulder at Dex before stretching up on her tiptoes to plant a kiss on my cheek. I smile and kiss her forehead, giving her a wink.

Dex makes a noise, but I ignore him.

"Night," I announce before heading to the bathroom.

Once I'm done, I creep down the hall, heading for Renzo's room. I quickly and quietly open the door, slip inside, and then enclose us in darkness as I shut it behind me.

"It's about time," he grumbles from the bed.

"It hasn't been that long. Your best friend was trying to question me."

"Question you about what?" he asks.

I start making my way to his side of the bed as I answer. "Just wanting to know more about me since I'm on this trip and haven't known any of you for as long as he has."

Renzo snorts, shifting to face me. "You'd think he was jealous."

I almost open my mouth to tell him he is, but it's not my place to tell him that his best friend is crushing on his sister. That's another conversation for another person, and I definitely don't want to be involved.

"Well, you are pretty okay looking."

Renzo sits up quickly and has his hands on my hips. "Pretty okay looking," he says with a chuckle, starting to undo my pants. "I'm pretty okay at sucking cock too. Let me show you."

"Oh, you're much better than pretty okay," I breathe.

He doesn't respond with words, he just shoves my pants and underwear down and takes my dick in his hand before wrapping his lips around me.

"Ohhh. Oh yes," I moan, twisting my fingers in his hair as he sucks me deep into his mouth.

After a few minutes, he grabs a hold of me and all but tosses me on the bed as he pushes his underwear down, climbing over me.

"You have no idea how bad I want to be in your ass right now." He punctuates the statement by letting his cock prod between my cheeks.

"Ahh," I moan, tossing my head back as I grip his biceps.

"But I know you're not ready."

"Maybe I am," I say, meeting his gaze.

His lips draw up. "Baby, you're not ready." His heavy cock slides against mine as he moves his body. "I wish you were, and I'll help you get there, but now's not the best time."

I whimper as he kisses my neck, grinding against me. "So, what are we gonna do?

Renzo reaches under the pillow and holds a square package in front of my face. "You're gonna fuck me."

"Wait, what? Where did you get a condom from?"

"I found it in Dex's room. He's not gonna need a fucking condom here, but he always has them on him."

I bite down on my lip, a smile growing. "Okay."

"Okay."

Renzo reaches back under the pillow and pulls out a small bottle of lube.

"Someone was sure I was going to come in here tonight."

"I'm also sure someone's gonna come in me tonight," he replies with a grin as he strokes my cock with his lubed up hand.

He squirts more onto his fingers and reaches around and begins to prepare himself.

"Holy shit," I whisper. "Why are you so fucking sexy?"

He grins, then strokes my cock again with his free hand.

"Okay, I can't wait anymore," he says, ripping the package open and rolling the latex over my length before straddling my hips and slowly lowering himself onto my cock.

"Shit," I hiss, pressing my fingers into the flesh on his waist as I hold on for dear life. "Oh fuck."

"Mm," he grunts, taking more of me inside.

"So tight," I breathe. "Oh my God."

Renzo fully seats himself on me and rotates his hips a little. "Fuck, Prep," he says. "I'm never gonna get enough of this."

My entire body is on fire. My cheeks and chest feel warm, and my heart bangs against my ribcage like it's dying to get away from the inferno happening inside me.

He rocks back and forth before rising up and dropping back down.

"Oh my...holy shit." I squeeze his hips at the same time I squeeze my eyes closed.

You never really know what to expect the first time you have sex, but this has got to be the best first experience to have.

"Renzo," I pant. "Oh my God."

He moves quicker now, sliding up and down my cock as he leans over me, his arms braced on either side of me.

With his mouth next to my ear, he makes the sexiest fucking noise—a mix between a pleasure-filled groan and a growl.

I wrap my arms around his back, pulling him lower, and then I claim his mouth with mine. The kiss is frenzied—messy and desperate, but I don't care. I want to taste him and swallow his moans as he rides my cock.

Renzo pulls away, sitting up while his hands rest on my stomach. His head drops back and my eyes track the lines of his neck, all the way down his sculpted abs, and finally land on his thick erection. I instantly reach out and grab it, my thumb smearing the small amount of pre-cum over his head before I stroke him.

"Shit," he moans. "Yeah, baby."

My hand moves quicker as he closes his eyes, moving up and down on my cock.

"I'm not gonna last much longer," I admit. "This is unreal."

Renzo stops moving, using the tip of his finger to swipe some of his arousal from around his slit before extending his hand to my mouth. I suck on his finger without hesitation, ripping a gravely groan from his throat.

He places his fists on either side of me, his cock pressed against my stomach as he moves with an energetic pace. My cock dips in and out of his ass, and I can barely keep my eyes open to watch him move, because seeing his muscles flex, his cock glide over my abs, and his beautiful face is too much to take.

"I'm about to come," I breathe, holding onto his thighs. "It's too good. Oh my God."

"Come, baby," he grunts. "Come in my ass."

"Oh shit!"

I squeeze him so hard I'm sure he'll have fingertip shaped bruises on his legs, but he keeps moving, unaffected.

"Fuck." He moves, grabbing his dick, and gives it a few strokes before he's coming all over my stomach.

"Jesus fucking Christ," I manage to say, my body going limp.

Renzo releases a long breath. "You're telling me. Your cock is perfect."

I bite down on my lip, and if I wasn't already flushed, my cheeks would turn red with his compliment. "I'm just glad you knew what you were doing, because my brain was misfiring and all I could think about was how good it felt. I wouldn't have been able to think about the logistics."

He chuckles, slowly getting off me. "Well, that makes sense, considering it was your first time. You'll never forget me now," he teases with a wink.

Renzo removes the condom from my shaft and ties it in a knot before tossing it in the trash can near his bed.

"Are you sore?" I ask.

"A little. It happens, but I'm a big boy. I'll be okay."

"Fuck," I breathe. "I can't believe how good that was. I don't even want to move right now."

He climbs in bed next to me. "I wish you could stay."

I turn my head and give him a lopsided grin. "I know. I'm sorry."

He waves me off. "So, you're not a virgin anymore. My corruption begins."

I laugh. "You can keep corrupting me if you want."

"Oh, I will," he says with a laugh, coming in for a kiss. "Because technically, I guess you're still a virgin in another way."

"Oh. Yeah."

He chuckles. "Oh yeah." He presses his naked body

against mine, his hand traveling across my hip. " I can't wait to claim that ass."

"Claim it?" I ask with a smirk.

"Yes, claim it. It will be mine, and you'll love every single thing I do to it."

"Mm."

His eyes drop to my mouth. "Fuck, you're too pretty."

"Pretty?"

"It's not a bad thing," he says, running his finger along my jawline. "You are pretty, and you're sexy, and you're irresistible. You're everything I've been looking for."

As if he wasn't meaning to say the last part, his eyes quickly snap to mine with a little trepidation behind them. His lips part, ready to come up with an explanation.

"And you're pretty okay looking," I say with a grin.

He starts laughing, and I have to hold my hand over his mouth, but it was all I wanted. He was feeling awkward with his admission, and instead of letting the moment get heavy, I gave him an out. I won't lie, though, it made my heart skip a beat, because I can't imagine being what he's always looked for. He's the perfect one. I'm just lucky to have found him exactly when I needed to.

"Shh," I say, trying to keep myself from laughing. "We don't need Dex coming in here."

He takes my hand from his mouth and kisses the back of it. "Okay, I'll shut up."

We lie next to each other for a while, lost in post-coital bliss. "I guess I should go," I say, moving to get up.

"Yeah. Okay."

I find my clothes and get dressed, and Renzo walks me to the door in all his naked glory.

"See you tomorrow," I say.

He locks his fingers with mine and grins. "See you tomorrow."

Renzo cracks the door open, staying behind it. I put my foot through the door, about to leave, though I'm not ready. Then I lean back in and kiss his lips.

"Bye."

He chuckles. "Bye."

When I close the door behind me, I can't wipe the grin off my face. I turn to make my way to my bedroom and spot Dex in the middle of the hall, looking right at me.

$$Chapter\ Twenty\text{-}Five$$

HE COCKS HIS HEAD, the creases between his brows deep. I take a breath and walk toward him, but I'm not the first to speak.

"What the fuck was that?" he spits, keeping his voice low.

I can either act stupid or tell the truth, but I know lying about this isn't going to work for a couple reasons. The first being that it was pretty obvious what just happened. I have no doubt he saw me lean back in to kiss who can only be Renzo on the other side of the door, leaving his room with a stupid, giddy smile. And the second being, if me and Renzo want to be together, Dex would find out anyway, so I might as well tell him and get it over with it. This is just another step to freeing myself.

"Probably what you think it was, but look..."

He cuts me off, stepping up to me. "No, what the fuck is going on? You're fucking around with Zo? Behind Vi's back? Both of you are fucked up. Move, we're gonna fucking settle this now," he says, pushing me to the side to storm toward Renzo's room.

I grab his arm, halting his steps. "Wait. If you're gonna try to be all high and mighty, then you be sure to tell Renzo that you're trying to move in on his sister."

He slowly spins in my direction, surprise showcased through his wide eyes and lifted brows. "What are you talking about?"

"You know exactly what I'm talking about." I put my hands in my pockets. "I know you were trying to touch Vi's ass at her parents' cabin, and then kissed her before she went to bed. I wonder how Renzo would feel about that, considering you yourself were just saying you're like family."

His jaw clenches as he crosses his arms over his chest. "I take it she told you this."

"Of course."

"So, you two aren't really together?"

"No, and she knows about me and Renzo, but look, nobody else knows about me."

He blows out a breath. "Hm. Okay."

"You can talk to Renzo about this later if you want, but Violet's fine with us. I'm not out, and eventually I'll do that on my terms, so I'd appreciate it if you didn't say anything to anybody."

Dex chews on his lip before nodding once. "Yeah, okay. Just don't tell Zo about me and Vi. Not that there is a me and Vi, but I just think if anything happens, I should tell him."

"I think before anything happens you should tell him."

He nods. "You're right. I'm just not sure anything will happen."

"I think she's confused, but honestly, she didn't say much," I tell him. "But now that you know, I'm gonna..." I jerk my thumb toward Renzo's door. "No point in sneaking now."

Dex snorts, his lips turning up at one end. "I swear this is only gonna inflate his ego even more. Pulling his sister's straight boyfriend."

"I'm not..."

"I know, but that's the story he'll tell, and honestly, I'm not surprised. He already told us he was crushing, and as long as a guy is willing, Zo will always be able to seal the deal."

I start smiling when he says Renzo already admitted to having a crush on me, but the second half of his statement makes my stomach roll. I'm still not sure why Renzo would want me if he can have anybody.

"Anyway," he says, shaking his head. "See y'all tomorrow."

"Yeah. Okay."

I enter Renzo's room again and see the light on in the bathroom, so I take a seat on the bed and wait for him.

A few minutes later he struts out wearing only a pair of boxer-briefs. He stops short when he sees me.

"Shit, you scared me." He chuckles. "What's up?"

"Dex knows."

His brows pull together. "Knows...what?"

"About us," I answer, a small grin growing.

"What?" he exclaims, coming closer.

"I ran into him as soon as I left earlier. There wasn't any covering up what was going on, and I figured I should tell him anyway. He's your best friend. He'd know eventually, right?"

Renzo smiles a heartstopping smile. "Yeah." He pulls me up and cradles my face, kissing my lips. "So we don't have to sneak around him anymore."

"Which is why I'm here again."

"Well, that makes me happy."

"You'll probably have to talk to him about it tomorrow, but—"

"I don't care. Get in the bed. Let's cuddle."

I laugh. "Let me use the bathroom first."

He smacks my ass as I walk away. "Hurry up."

Chapter Twenty-Six

"MORNING, SLEEPY HEAD." Renzo's voice is laced with humor as he runs his fingers through my hair as he kneels next to the bed.

I blink several times before I speak. "What time is it? Did I sleep in?"

"Nah. I'm up early." He stands and shoves his phone in his pocket. "I'm gonna talk to Dex before my parents show up."

"Oh okay." I push the cover down a little before I stretch. "I'll start getting ready so I'm not naked in your bed when they get here."

"Good call," he says with a crooked grin before strutting out of the room.

I wait a few minutes before I climb out from under the covers, then I grab my clothes and drape them over my arm before I head to my own room.

On my way past the doorway to the living room, I begin to hear voices, and though it's not my intention to eavesdrop, I can't help but pick up a few things.

"You fucking dog," Dex laughs. "Your sister's boyfriend?"

"They weren't really dating," Renzo says. "But I told you I wanted him."

"Yeah, you always love the innocent ones," he says with another laugh. "Now what? This is supposed to be serious? He's in the closet, Zo. That's not really your thing."

"I know."

My pulse jumps as I wait to see what he'll say next, and as bad as I feel for listening in on their conversation, I need to know what he's gonna say next.

"I don't know much about the guy," Dex says. "He seems okay, but let's be real. You're just out of a relationship and from what I've seen you've really been enjoying the single life. So, is this just a hook-up while we're out here? Or do I need to start forming a relationship with the guy because he'll be around?"

I press myself closer to the wall, my heart climbing up my throat. I don't even know what I want his answer to be. I guess a big part of me wants him to say he's serious about me —that I'm not just someone to fuck and leave. However, I'm also very aware of our situation, and I already know he's not into hiding anything about himself. Unless I come out immediately, I worry how long he'll even wait.

"I really like him," Renzo says, the words coming out slow like it was hard for him to admit. "I don't want to rush him into coming out, because that's not fair to him."

"But it's not fair to you to hide a relationship."

"I know, I know. Look, it's not serious right now. It's fine. We're having fun. I don't know what's gonna happen, but...."

I hurry down the hall toward my room to pick up new clothes before I head to the bathroom to take a shower.

While the water washes over me, I can't stop twirling Renzo's statements around in my head. He likes me, which isn't new information, and he didn't say it was just a fling, so that might mean he could want more.

I scrub my head, trying to keep myself from overthinking. We've been messing around for just a few days. Nobody's ready to settle down in such a short time, so me and Renzo should be fine for a while. We can mess around in private while we determine what the hell we want with each other.

Doing my best to ignore the fact that he's been with a closeted person and that didn't work out, and that both his mom and best friend have made comments about how doing that again wouldn't be a good idea, I get out of the shower and start getting dressed.

Of course I want to continue whatever it is we're doing, but every time I think about being out in public with him and holding his hand or kissing him, fear seizes my heart and I worry what people will think. I'm not sure I'm thick-skinned enough to let their dirty looks or whispered comments not affect me. Especially if it's people we go to school with and live around. It's not like here, where I'll likely never see these people again.

Deep down I know I shouldn't care, but it's always easy to say that. *I don't care what they think.* It's different to actually mean it. I think half the people who say that really do care. It's normal to fear being judged, right? We want people to like us.

I let out a low growl, frustrated with myself and my thoughts. Why would I care if some homophobic asshole didn't like me?

But what if that homophobic asshole is my dad? Or my mom? It always comes back to them, because even if Renzo and his close group of friends made it easy for me to be me, I always have to worry about telling my parents, and that's when the real fear sets in.

Once I'm done doing everything I need to do, I yank open the door and almost plow into Violet.

"Sorry," I murmur, ready to move past her and into my room.

"Uh-uh," she says, planting her hand on my chest and pushing me back into the bathroom. "What's going on?"

"How do you figure something's going on?" I ask.

"Your inner thoughts are almost as loud as mine."

I cock my head, but she purses her lips and gives me a look that let's me know she's not stupid and isn't willing to let this go.

I sigh and lean against the sink. "Just thinking."

"Duh. I just said that. What about?"

"Just everything. Me and Renzo. Me coming out. That kind of stuff."

"I thought everything was fine? I heard there was a sleep-over last night," she says with a small grin.

"Yeah, I mean, everything is fine. It's just I've heard your mom and Dex mention how Renzo shouldn't try anything with a person who wasn't out yet. Plus, he told me the story about what happened when he did try that before, and I feel bad putting him back in that position."

"Renzo will only do what he wants to do. If he's willing to keep this a secret for a while, he will."

"And when he's no longer willing to do that?"

Violet frowns. "Then you'll know."

I rub a hand over my face. "I feel better now that you and Dex know, but I knew beforehand that you two weren't going to be judgemental considering he's your brother and Dex's best friend. Not everyone is so accepting."

"People suck, and yeah, there will be people who don't like that you're gay, but you know what? People will find something to hate no matter what. I've had girls hate me because their boyfriends liked me. Not that I was flirting with them, or that I liked them, but that the boys liked me. How is that my fault?" She shakes her head and rolls her eyes. "I know people think I'm a stuck-up, conceited bitch, but honestly, I'm not. I have my own set of insecurities people don't know about, and I can't change their opinions about me. I used to go out of my way to be nice and friendly, but they don't like that either, so fuck 'em."

I crack a smile. "You make it sound simple."

"It's not. I know. But, Ronan, you can't do anything about the fact that you're gay. You can spend your whole life lying and trapped in the closet, but that means you'll never love and you'll never live. Not to be all, *Live, Laugh, Love,*" she says with a giggle.

"I know, but eventually I'll have to tell my family."

She frowns. "They wouldn't accept you?"

I shake my head. "I have a hard time thinking they'd be okay with it. I've heard their comments before. Being gay is wrong and they don't know why people make the conscious decision to go against what's natural."

Violet's face shifts from sadness to outrage. "That's fucked up. They don't have the authority to judge people." She curls a lock of hair behind her ear and tilts her head. "Maybe they'd feel different with their son."

I shake my head slightly. "I don't know about that."

"Well, give them a chance. Renzo was worried about telling our parents, too. They might be okay, but even if they aren't, at least you don't still live with them. You're out here with us, and we can be your family. It'll be their loss and our gain."

I smile wide. "I appreciate that. Thank you."

"You're welcome," she says with a sweet grin.

"Now, what's going on with you?"

She waves her hand through the air. "Only about sixty-million things."

A knock on the door pauses our conversation.

"Hello?" Renzo's voice calls out.

Violet pulls open the door. "Yes?"

His eyes bounce between us. "If I didn't know any better, I'd be worried about finding you two in a bathroom."

Violet rolls her eyes and I push away from the sink. "We were just talking."

Renzo smirks. "Figured it wasn't much more than that. You okay?" He walks in and grabs my hand.

"I'm gonna go," Violet says, stepping through the door.

"I'm fine," I answer, but aren't those the cliché words you say when you're not fine?

Renzo studies my face, searching for the lie. "You sure?"

I kiss his soft lips. "I'm sure. Let's go eat."

I refuse to spend the rest of our time here worrying about what could happen in the future. I'm gonna take Violet's advice and live. I'll worry about the rest when the time comes.

"Well, you look good enough to eat," Renzo flirts, coming in for another kiss while his hands travel under my shirt.

"Hello? We're here!"

Renzo groans. "There goes my erection. Mom and her perfect timing."

I chuckle before he devours my mouth with a sensual kiss that'll have to last us until his parents leave.

Renzo

Chapter Twenty-Seven

THE TIME UP here in the cabins, away from our usual day-to-day routines has been the best time I've had in a long time.

As usual, we didn't exchange presents for Christmas. As of three or four years ago, the tradition has always been to travel for Christmas break, and once we're back home, we exchange gifts on New Year's Eve. However, we did have a huge Christmas dinner.

I'll never forget Ronan's words to me once we had climbed into bed that night.

"That was the best Christmas I can remember having."

Something as simple as a dinner with family and friends was his best Christmas. He later told me that since he was nine or ten, the typical traditions had come to an end. His parents didn't put forth a lot of effort once he found out Santa wasn't real. They'd give him a present or two, but nothing kids typically want. No toys, just clothes or a book.

"Don't get me wrong, I loved reading," he had said, not wanting to sound ungrateful.

I know we should be appreciative to get even simple

things, and that a lot of kids aren't able to receive anything, but I can't help but want to make up for the years he missed out on. I always looked forward to Christmas as a kid because my parents went all out. The entire house is always decorated like a winter wonderland, and we'd always have a huge dinner with family and friends. Then when we became teens, we always looked forward to the trips we'd take, and the present exchange right before the new year.

Now it's the day before we head home, and I feel this growing sense of dread in the pit of my stomach. Everything's been perfect out here. My parents still aren't aware of our new situation, but every time they'd go back to their cabin, we'd be able to comfortably be ourselves.

He and Dex have gotten a little closer, and we've all had a lot of fun together, whether it was just pool games, drinking games, or skiing and sledding outside.

Back at home, we won't be near each other as often anymore, and when we are, I'll be forced to keep my hands to myself and wait until we can sneak off and have some alone time. I worry things between us will change when we get back, but I'm trying to be cautiously optimistic.

"So, you're coming to our house on New Year's Eve, right?" I ask, my arm draped around his shoulders as we sit on the couch.

"That's when you guys exchange gifts?"

"Yep."

"I don't know. I don't want to intrude on a family tradition."

"It's not a formal, family only thing," I assure him. "Sometime's Vi's friends come over, and Dex has been there a handful of times, too."

"Yeah. Okay, maybe."

I squeeze his shoulder playfully. "I'll take that as a yes."

"Just give in," Vi tells him as she walks by, heading to the kitchen. "It'll be fun. I've already invited Scarlet and Monique. Did you invite anyone else, Zo?"

"I'll be there," Dex announces from the dining room table as he plays Solitaire.

"Jayden and Trevor are gonna stop by."

"Trevor? Really?" she questions, her eyes sliding from me to Ronan.

"We basically plan these things months out. You know that."

"Yeah, but..."

I give her a look to leave it alone, considering Dex doesn't know about Trevor either.

"Who's Trevor?" Ronan asks.

Fuck.

"He was at the party at their house," Dex chimes in.

"I didn't really know anybody but Violet at that party."

"He's been a close friend of ours for a long time, too," Dex continues. "Why don't you want him there?" He aims the question at Vi.

She fiddles with her fingers. "Oh, it's not that. I just thought y'all had a fight or something. I don't know. Maybe I'm confused." She lets out a nervous laugh before sticking her head in the fridge.

I feel Ronan's eyes on me, so I angle my head to meet his gaze. "He was the one in the basement," I say softly.

It takes a second to click, but when it does, his eyebrows jump up and his eyes widen a little. "Oh. Ohh."

"It's not a big deal."

I can feel the change in his energy, but he forces a smile and nods. "Okay."

"I can tell you more later," I say, angling my body toward him and blocking Dex from being able to watch my mouth as I say, "He's not out." The words are barely a whisper as they leave my lips.

Ronan's eyes double in size again. "Oh. Okay."

"Shuffle those up. Let's play something else," Vi says, pulling a chair out at the dining room table. "Guys?"

"Yeah, let's do it," I say, standing up.

~

We wake up at an ungodly hour, at my parents' behest, leaving the sanctuary of our cabin behind, and eat breakfast at a diner before we actually hit the road to head back home.

After convincing my dad that we know the way back, we're able to persuade them to start their journey before we even leave the restaurant. They think it's because I wanted to order more food, but it's because I want to be able to ride back with Ronan without them asking questions.

"So, who's taking which car?" Vi asks. "You two both drove up here. Me and Dex are just the passengers."

"Well, you're definitely not driving my car," I say, earning an eye roll.

Dex chuckles. "I can drive your car back home, man. You can ride with Ronan in his. We can just meet up at the school when we get back in town."

I look at Ronan who nods. "Sounds good to me."

"Well, you can be in control of the car, but I'm in control of the music," Violet tells Dex.

"Fine," he grumbles.

"Looks like you're giving me another ride," I whisper into Ronan's ear.

His cheeks flush that beautiful shade of pink I love so much as he grips my thigh under the table.

Chapter Twenty-Eight

WE'VE BEEN BACK in town for four days, and today is New Year's Eve, so I'll finally be able to hang out with Ronan for an extended amount of time. We've seen each other a few times since we've been back, but never for long, and almost never just the two of us.

Once was at the pizza parlor, but that was kind of a bust because it was crowded, including Jayden and Bryant again. That was awkward, to say the least.

The second time was when I invited him over to the house, thinking my parents were gonna be gone for a few hours, only for them to show back up thirty minutes after they left. Vi put on a movie and pretended like that was the plan all along, but of course my mom was interested in the movie and stayed in the living room with us the whole time.

The third time was better, since I was able to take him out to the lake I usually go to when I want to canoe. Because it's cold and partially frozen, we stayed in the car, but at least it was time for just us, and we were able to fool around a little.

"Morning, dear," Mom greets as she pours a cup of coffee.

"Morning."

161

"You okay?" she questions, cupping the mug between both hands as she watches me.

I pull open the fridge. "Yeah, I'm fine. Why?"

"You haven't seemed like your usual cheery self since we've been back."

I take out the pitcher of lemonade and put it on the counter between us. "Really?" I shrug. "I guess I just miss it. It was a nice place, right?"

She studies me for a few seconds before she responds. "Yes it was. We'll have to go back sometime."

I hadn't realized my mood had shifted in such a way that my mom was questioning if I was all right. I mean, yeah, I wish I could hang out with Ronan more, especially since we're still out of school, but I hate that it's affecting me already. We haven't known each other that long.

I remove a glass from the cupboard, wanting to change the subject. "So, my friends are coming around eight. That okay?"

"Yeah, perfect," she replies, placing her mug down. "I think Vi said the same thing. Are you inviting anyone special?"

With a grin, I say, "Why? You expecting grandbabies soon? Because I hate to break it to you, I don't think that's gonna happen."

She scoffs. "Oh, stop. I'm just wondering."

"No, I won't be with anybody tonight," I reply, hating that that's the truth.

"Okay, well, I have to make a few calls, but I'll be back a little later to start on the food for tonight."

"Do you need help?"

"No, it's okay. It's not going to be anything big, just finger foods. Plus, your dad will help."

"Okay. Just let me know if you need me."

She walks past me and pats my shoulder. "I will."

After she disappears upstairs, Vi comes creeping down the same staircase.

"Mom gone?"

"Went to her room, I think."

"Okay, cool. She was harassing me earlier about what I'm gonna get Ronan for the present exchange, and I hadn't even thought about it, but now that I realize we still have to keep up pretenses, I don't know what the hell to get. What do you think?"

I chew on my bottom lip. "Well, I actually got him a few things."

"Really?" she exclaims with a squeaky voice. "Like what?"

"Don't worry about it, nosey."

"Ugh. Well, is there anything I can give him that won't be weird coming from me?"

"Just get him anything you'd get a friend. It's not a big deal."

"Mom always hates on the gifts I buy."

"Well, you did get Aunt Susan a basket of goodies with peanuts in almost every snack."

"It's not my fault she developed a peanut allergy."

I laugh. "She didn't just develop it last year, she's always had it."

"Ugh."

"And you can't forget the time you bought me lube and condoms."

"Hey! That's a great gift. It shows I care about your safety and health."

"I don't think Mom and Dad appreciated that you had me open it in front of their work colleagues, but don't get me wrong, it was a gift that was well used."

"Gross. Anyway, fine, I'm gonna head out and figure something out. I'll be back before everyone shows up."

"You only have a few hours, don't get caught up shopping

for yourself." She gives me a mischievous smile before walking toward the door. "And be careful. You just got the car back."

"Yeah, yeah. See you soon."

I take out my phone and text Ronan.

Can't wait to see you tonight.

I can't wait either. Wish it was just us though.

Oh? Having naughty thoughts about me?

Maybe...

That's nice to know. I think we need to rent a hotel room for a night so we can have some time to do...whatever we want.

When?

I'll arrange it and let you know.

I head to the shower with a smile on my face, ready for tonight and the coming days.

Chapter Twenty-Nine

DRESSED in a white button up and black slacks, I sip on some non-alcoholic drink Mom put out while I wait for everyone to show up.

We exchanged some of our bigger gifts already, but left some smaller ones to open up when everyone else arrives.

Vi's friends show up first, as usual, and after Scarlet and Monique drop off their gifts under the tree, the three of them disappear into Violet's room, giggling and texting other people.

Not too much later, the bell rings, bringing Dex, Trevor, and Jayden to the door.

"Happy New Year!" Jayden exclaims with his arms in the air as soon as he steps in.

"Not yet, Jayden," Mom calls from her seat in the living room. "How are you boys?"

"I'm good, Mrs. H," Jayden replies, heading in her direction. "How are my second favorite parents?"

Mom laughs as Dad grins, shaking his head. "We're doing good," Dad answers, shaking Jay's hand. "How're your parents?"

"They're good."

Dex waves at my parents. "Long time no see."

Mom waves him off with a smile, used to his sarcastic ways. "How was your Christmas, Trevor?"

"Oh, it was good. I heard you guys took a trip. Was it good?"

"Minus the blizzard and power outage, yes."

"Oh shit, a blizzard took out the power?" Trevor asks, lowering his voice as we head toward the kitchen to congregate around the island.

"Yeah. Me and Ronan got trapped in one cabin while Dex, Vi, and my parents were in another."

Trevor tries to hold in his laugh as he looks at Dex. "Bet that was fun."

Dex shrugs. "I didn't mind it too much."

"And you and Ronan? Vi's boyfriend? How did that go?"

Dex plays it cool and doesn't make a face or anything, so I try to keep it together just as well. "Yeah, it was fine. He's cool."

"Bet that was hard considering you've been lusting after him," Jayden says, slapping on my arm as he barks out a laugh.

"What? You have a crush on him?" Trevor asks.

"A crush on who?" Mom asks, walking into the kitchen with her empty wine glass.

"Nobody. Everybody." I grin and Mom shakes her head. "We're gonna head downstairs. Let me know when everyone's here."

"Will do."

In the basement, Dex and Jayden start setting up a pool game while Trevor hangs back with me.

"So, a crush on Vi's boyfriend?" He smiles, letting me know he's not judging me.

"It's not as weird as it sounds. They're not really together."

Trev chuckles. "Whatever you say, man."

I wait for it to be awkward between us, but it doesn't happen. I'm glad we were able to move past our hook-up without ruining our friendship.

"How are you?" I cut my eyes to the guys to make sure they aren't paying attention. "You know, with everything."

"Fine, I guess. I'm not really in denial, but I don't know how to move forward either."

"I get that."

I wish he and Ronan could talk to each other about this, because they have a lot in common, and it might help to know someone else is going through the same thing at the same time. While I had to tell Ronan about Trevor in order to keep him from saying something in front of Dex, I can't tell Trevor about Ronan.

Ten minutes later, me and Trevor are bowled over, laughing at the fact that Jayden somehow managed to skip a ball off the table and hit Dex right in his nuts when Ronan appears at the bottom of the steps.

"Hey!" I realize my voice sounds too excited, so I tone it down before I continue. "What's up?"

He gives me a half grin. "Your mom told me to bring you guys up. There's a few people out there already, plus some guy who arrived when I did."

"Okay, cool."

With my back turned to the rest of the guys, I allow my eyes to travel up and down his body, loving how good he looks. He's wearing a solid gray cardigan sweater over a white button-up with a pair of dark denim jeans and dress shoes.

He turns around as soon as I start to see the blush bloom in his cheeks.

Trevor taps me on the shoulder, so I angle my head to see him. "I get it," he says simply.

I laugh as I head up the stairs, but come to a screeching halt as soon as I spot Kris.

"What the fuck?" Dex says as soon as he notices him. He spins to look at me, bewilderment changing his features.

"I have no idea," I reply.

Jayden and Trevor both know him, too, and they both watch me for a reaction.

"Is that who came in with you?" I ask Ronan.

"Yeah, why?"

"That's my ex."

Kris finds me and smiles, strutting directly to me.

Ronan

Chapter Thirty

I WATCH as the attractive guy I walked in with struts toward Renzo with all the confidence in the world. His smile is bright, reaching his eyes, and his arms are outstretched, waiting to wrap themselves around Renzo's body.

He's the epitome of tall, dark, and handsome. His dark curly hair looks soft and shiny, and his skin is a flawless shade of light brown. The line of his jaw is sharp, covered by just a smattering of hair.

"Renzo," he says, his voice as smooth as butter. "It's so good to see you."

He sounds genuine as he wraps him in a tight hug—an intimate hug. My heart clenches at the sight, because if I'm honest, they look great together.

"What are you doing here?" Renzo questions, stepping out of the hug.

Kris is sure to hold on to his hands as he continues to stare at him. "Your mom invited me, and I'm so glad she did. We have a lot to talk about, and what better time to have a clean slate than New Years."

He smiles wide again, forgetting about everyone around them.

"Hey guys," he says, talking to Dex, Trevor, and Jayden. "How's it going?"

They each mumble a response, unsure how to react to him considering the history with Renzo. Kris's gaze finally lays on me and gives me a once over before grinning.

"Who's this?"

"Ronan," I offer, giving him my hand.

He slips his hand into mine and shakes it. "You new?"

"He's dating Vi," Jayden says.

"Oh. Okay." He faces Renzo and drags his knuckles over his cheek. "I'm gonna go say hi to your dad. I'll be back."

Once he's gone, Dex is the first to speak up. "What the fuck is that? He's just acting like everything's cool? Have you talked to him since y'all broke up?"

"Not once," Renzo says, staring at Kris as he makes his way through the living room. "Apparently my mom is trying to get us back together."

"And he's all touching you and shit," Dex continues. "I'd be pissed if I were..." His eyes find mine, but he catches himself and says, "You," as he looks back at Renzo.

"He did say he just needed a break," Jayden pipes in. "Maybe he's ready to settle down now."

"Come on, everybody!" Renzo's mom announces, calling us to the tree.

The guys head over, but I stay behind with Renzo when I notice he doesn't bother to take a step. He watches me, ready for me to say something, but there's nothing to be said.

"I really had no idea he'd be here."

"I know."

He begins to reach out for my hand but stops himself. "I'm sorry."

I try to shrug it off, but my stomach is in knots. Will he

realize he still loves him? Will Renzo want another chance with the one guy he's loved? Could I blame him? "It's okay. Don't worry about it."

We head toward the tree and everyone starts exchanging gifts. Violet and her friends pass each other boxes while Jayden tosses Trevor a badly wrapped gift.

Renzo's mom and dad open up gifts from each other, and then Violet comes over with a small red bag.

"I didn't know what to get you, but I hope you like it."

I crack a grin at her. "I'm sure I'll love it."

"Vi's notorious for giving bad gifts. Don't get your hopes up," Renzo says, appearing at my side.

"Shut up," she tells him, shoving a box in his chest. "Here's yours. Where's mine?"

Renzo chuckles before leaving to find her present, and I open the bag. I reach in and pull out a book, but as soon as I read the title I shove it back in the bag. It's titled, *Yay for Gay!*

I start laughing as I pinch the bag closed. "Thanks."

"What is it?" Renzo questions when he returns. I hand him the bag and once he gets a look, he starts laughing, too. "Good lord, Vi."

"What? I thought it was good."

"It is. I appreciate it, thank you," I tell her, giving her a hug.

"Not for now, in front of all these people," Renzo says with a chuckle.

"Whatever. Present?" she says, holding her hand out as soon as we disengage.

Renzo hands her a box, and I bend down and pick up the one I got for her and put it on top of his.

"Merry New Year."

"Thanks, boys," she says with a smile, heading back to her friends.

Renzo and I are quiet for a few seconds, but then he

barely nudges my elbow to get my attention. "I got you something, too."

I bite down on my grin. "I have something for you too. I wasn't really sure if I should bring it or not, but—"

"It's okay," he says. "We can exchange later."

"Surprise!" Renzo's mom yells, a wine glass in one hand and the other hand around Kris's waist. "I thought it would be nice for you two to spend some time together."

Another megawatt smile splits Kris's face as he squeezes Renzo's mom's shoulders. "I love this woman."

Renzo slips his hands in his pockets. "Yeah, it is quite the surprise, considering he seemed to disappear a few months back."

"Lorenzo, be nice," his mom chides. "He came here to see you."

"It's okay, Mrs. Hayes, I'll get him to come around."

Kris's eyes sparkle when they land on Renzo, and I hate the confidence he has, like he knows it's only a matter of time before Renzo succumbs to his charm.

"Have fun, boys," she says before wandering off.

"I got you a drink," Kris says, handing Renzo a glass.

"Yeah, I need one," he responds, taking the glass and sipping from it. "Oh, that's good."

"I know how you like it," Kris flirts.

Renzo's eyes shoot over to me, and I suddenly feel like a third wheel so I take off toward Violet.

Dex grabs my arm before I get to her. "Don't stress over that, man. I don't think Zo will fall for his shit again."

"It hasn't been that long."

"I know, but..." He studies Renzo and Kris, the closeness of their bodies and the familiar way they interact. He sighs. "Just know I'm on your team."

I try to force a grin. "Thanks."

~

A couple hours later, I'm sitting in the corner of the couch with a drink in my hand. Dex has been spiking our drinks without Renzo's parents knowing, and I'm starting to feel a little better, especially considering I've had to watch Kris attach himself to Renzo's ass all night.

Kris was sure to get everyone's attention when he presented Renzo with his gift—a framed photo of the night sky on the night they had their first date. He also had some speech prepared about how he can never look up at the stars without thinking about him.

Most everyone swooned over the gesture, but Dex and Vi both gave me pity glances. I can tell Kris is doing his best to get back in Renzo's good graces, but I'm trying to keep the fear and dread at bay, because besides a couple hugs and a few shared laughs, Renzo hasn't done much to show he's into Kris like that.

However, Kris has monopolized most of Renzo's time, so I've hardly talked to him at all tonight, but he hasn't talked to the other guys either.

"I remember why I didn't like Kris that much," Trevor says, dropping next to me. "He's sort of controlling."

"What do you mean?" I ask.

"He always had Zo like this," he says, gesturing at them. "Away from everyone."

"He wants him to himself."

"Yeah, but not in a cute way. He doesn't want Renzo to be around anyone else."

"Were you friends with Kris before?"

He makes a face. "Not really. We didn't know him until Renzo brought him around. He seemed cool at first, and don't get me wrong, he'll never come off like a bad guy, but there's something about him, just lingering under the surface. You know?"

"I suppose."

"I know you haven't known Zo very long, but he's someone who shines brightly. He walks into a room and you know he's there without even seeing him. He talks to you and you feel special, like he really cares about what you're going through. He's one of the best people I know, but there has been a slight shift in him when he's been in a relationship. Luke and Kris affected him."

"Luke is the one who was in the closet?"

"Yep. Renzo dimmed a little when he was with these guys. It's like he loves and cares so deeply that he allows the person he's with to change him because he thinks it will help the other one, or help them as a couple."

I watch Trevor's face as he stares at Kris and Renzo across the room, and I can tell he really cares about him.

"You like him," I say.

He snaps his head in my direction, his face tense as his eyes pierce mine. "What?"

I know it's not my place to talk about his sexuality, but because I know and because I feel like I need someone to talk to, and perhaps, more than anything else, because alcohol is running through my bloodstream, I say, "*I* like him."

His brows furrow. "You what?"

"I'm gay. Nobody really knows."

His almond shaped green eyes widen slightly. "What?"

"Please don't tell anyone."

"Umm. Sorry, I'm just a little..." He shakes his head, staring down at the carpet. "You like Renzo?"

"It's sort of a long story," I reply.

Trevor glances around before meeting my gaze. "Can we go talk?"

"Yeah, sure."

Chapter Thirty-One

TWO THINGS HAPPEN as me and Trevor cut through the living room, heading for the basement. Mr. Hayes presents his wife with one last gift—a week-long trip to West Virginia to see her sister, which has them leaving tomorrow. The second thing to happen is overhearing Kris instantly tell Renzo that means he can stay here for that week, so they can get reacquainted.

Renzo doesn't notice me and Trevor walk by, and luckily, we're gone before I can hear his response.

In the basement, Trevor heads to the small bar in the corner and grabs a bottle of liquor and pours two shots. He raises one to me, his brows raised in question.

"Fuck it," I say, taking it and swallowing it down.

He does the same before sucking in a deep breath. "I'm gay, too." I don't want to say I know already, so I simply nod my head. "I had been questioning what was wrong with me. I wasn't interested in all the chicks who would basically be throwing themselves at me at the frat house parties. And uhh..." he scratches the back of his head, looking down. "Well, maybe a month ago now, I got really drunk and me and Zo kinda messed around."

I try not to react, but it still stings, even though I know I wasn't even in the picture then. "What happened?"

"I fucked up. I acted like a real asshole and pretended I didn't remember, but the truth is I was terrified. I had finally caved. I did what I had been curious about for a while. Renzo was confused when I kissed him, but I didn't allow him to question it, I just kept drunkenly kissing him and things progressed a little farther, but the next day I woke up and was embarrassed. I felt like I had used my best friend, and I didn't want to have the conversation about what that meant."

"I get that."

"Anyway, the next party I had, I made sure to get drunk and made out with several girls, hoping it would ignite a feeling in me that was similar to what I felt with Renzo, but it didn't. I've hooked up with girls before, but it never felt right. You know?" He takes a breath. "Anyway, me and Zo talked it out and got past it. He said we should probably preserve our friendship, which I agree with, but it was a real eye opener for me. None of our other friends know, and I'm not even sure how to start telling people."

"You and me both," I say, taking the bottle and pouring us a couple more shots. "But it's nice to have someone to talk to."

We clink our glasses and down the clear liquid. "Just so you know, I don't have strong romantic feelings for Renzo. Being with him was exciting because he's a guy, not because he's him. You know?"

I nod. "Yeah, I understand."

"So, you're afraid to come out, too?"

"My family won't accept me. I know where they stand."

"I'm not really sure about my parents," he admits.

"Me and Zo have already started messing around," I tell

him. "I know that's weird to tell you now, since you just told me about your experience with him."

Trevor laughs. "Fucking whorebag Lorenzo."

Feeling tipsy, I laugh too, probably for longer than necessary. "I do really like him, and I think he likes me too, but I was already concerned about what might happen. I know about Luke, and I know his mom and Dex didn't want him to be with someone who wasn't out yet. And now, with what you just told me, I don't want to be another person to dim his light."

Trevor frowns. "Sorry, man."

I shrug, leaning over the bar. "I know it's in my hands. I know we could have a better chance if I were to just come out and be willing to be with him in public without fear. At least until now...now I have to worry about him getting back with Kris."

"Ugh. With that cheesy ass gift and speech?" he says, making a face.

"Renzo loved him."

"Past tense."

"He still might."

He's quiet for a few beats. "Don't give him time to fall back in love with him. Don't let him think Kris is the only person for him."

"What do I do?"

He shrugs. "Only you know."

Not much later, Vi and her friends, along with the rest of the guys, minus Renzo and Kris, come down to the basement.

"Was Kris down here?" Vi asks me.

"No, why?"

"I thought I saw him coming from this direction when we were heading over."

I shrug. "Maybe he was in the kitchen."

"Have you talked to Renzo?" she asks, a partial frown on her lips.

"Not since when we were by the tree."

She sighs. "You know, I thought he was happy with Kris because we rarely saw him, but I'm wondering if that's just because Kris likes to keep him to himself. I get wanting to spend time with someone you're in a relationship with, but if they're keeping you from friends and family, that's a bit much."

"Trevor mentioned something similar," I say.

"Where the fuck is Zo?" Jayden questions, pool stick in hand as he glances around the room. "He should be down here."

"With Kris," Dex mumbles.

"Fuck that. He's gonna bring his ass down here," he says, marching toward the stairs.

"Renzo really wanted you to have a good time tonight. He kept talking about it. I'm sorry it ended up like this," Vi tells me, resting her head on my arm as we lean against the bar.

"It's okay."

"I can't find him," Jayden says as soon as he hits the bottom step. "You think he dipped out with Kris?"

"I swear to God," Vi says, unlocking her phone and clicking on the messages app. After a couple minutes, she huffs. "He's not answering them."

"Give him a minute. Not everybody responds to texts in thirty seconds like you girls do," Dex says.

Violet narrows her eyes at him. "He always answers my texts."

"It's gonna be midnight in half an hour," Trevor says. "It's not like him to miss that. I'm sure he'll be back."

My stomach rolls, the alcohol sloshing around as I think about what he and Kris could be doing right now. I didn't come here thinking we'd have some romantic moment as the clock struck midnight, but I had hoped we'd at least be near each other.

"I think I'm gonna go," I say, pushing away from the counter.

"What? No!" Vi squeaks.

Jayden and Vi's friends look at me like I'm an asshole, and I remember they don't know the truth. They just think I'm abandoning my girlfriend right before midnight.

"I mean, I'm just gonna go get some air real quick. I'll be back." I plant a kiss on Vi's cheek before I head upstairs.

Mr. and Mrs. Hayes are on the couch talking to a couple of their friends, and I do my best to avoid eye contact as I make my way to the front door.

"You okay, dear?" Mrs. Hayes asks.

"Yes, ma'am. Just gonna grab something from my car real quick."

"Okay."

Outside, the cold air feels good against my heated flesh. The alcohol has me feeling warm, so I welcome the breeze.

I'm only on the porch for a couple minutes before the wind carries the low voices of two men to my ears. I can't make out the words, but I know it's Renzo and Kris, so when I step forward and look to the left, I'm not surprised to see them at the edge of the house, away from the lights and prying eyes. They both have their backs to me, so they aren't aware anyone came outside.

A minute later, the door behind me opens and I turn around and find Mr. Hayes coming to join me.

"Hey," he says quietly.

"Hi."

I haven't spoken to Mr. Hayes too much. He's a fairly

quiet man, but he's always been nice. However, this is the first time we've been alone together, so I'm unsure what to talk to him about. I'm supposed to be dating his daughter, but I'm lusting after his son, and I worry I'll say the wrong thing.

"Kinda cold out here, son."

"Yeah. I was gonna go in soon."

He stands next to me, staring out across their expansive yard, lit up with Christmas lights, his hands in his pockets. I glance at him, wondering why he came out here. Are we about to have the *what are your intentions with my daughter* talk?

Mr. Hayes hears a noise and turns in the direction of his son and Kris. He stares into the darkened corner for a few seconds before he looks back at me.

My heart seizes and either the cold or fear causes me to start trembling. I can tell by the look in his eyes that he's about to say something I'm not quite ready for. It's concern mixed with pity and a smidge of frustration.

"You know the saying *It's the quiet ones you have to watch out for?*" I nod, and he stares back toward the road. "I've always been quiet. Some people think that's rude or believe that means I'm stuck-up, but the truth of the matter is that I'm just a deep thinker and an observer. I enjoy sitting back and watching the world move around me. That's not to say I don't enjoy existing in that same world, but I like to know what's going on wherever I am.

"I pay attention to anything that involves my kids, and as much as they may hate that, I do it because I care about them. I want to make sure they're being safe and I like getting to know the people they hang out with because I want to feel comfortable when they're out away from me."

"Sir, I'm not a bad person," I say, starting to wonder what this conversation is actually about.

"I know. You seem like a good kid." He waits a few beats before looking back in the direction of Renzo and Kris. "My son loves deeply. It may not seem like it, but his feelings are always worn on his sleeves. He can't help but project what he's feeling or thinking. It radiates off of him. Violet is very similar. When she's happy, in love, angry, sad, you'll definitely know. She's not one to hide her feelings.

He turns and faces me. "If Violet was in love, I'd know. If she was infatuated, I would know. But the truth is she's not. Lorenzo on the other hand...well, I've never seen him happier than when we were up at the cabins. He was smiling nearly the entire time."

"Sir, I'm not sure I know what you mean." Beads of sweat form across my body, even out in the cold.

He grins and it's the same crooked smile Renzo has. "Don't let your emotions cloud your vision. Sit back and watch what's really happening around you. You may be surprised."

Mr. Hayes angles his body, giving me a view of Renzo and Kris. From what I can see, they're not touching, and the body language isn't romantic. If anything, they both seem tense. Maybe they're arguing.

"I may not know how certain things came to be, but if anyone is actually paying attention, it's obvious what's going on here." He drops his hand to my shoulder and gives it a slight squeeze. "Let's head inside."

I don't respond, I just follow him into the house, dumb-struck. I'm pretty sure he just told me in a round-about way that he knows about me and his son, and he's not angry about it either.

God, I wish I had been born into a family this accepting.

Renzo

Chapter Thirty-Two

"I DON'T CARE what you think you heard, I know you're lying, Kris. Why would you make that up?" I question, my fury keeping me from freezing out here in the cold.

"I was going to the basement to make a call away from the noise, and when I was partially down the stairs I overheard part of their conversation. What came next was obvious based on the noises."

"Earlier you said you saw Ronan and Trevor making out, now it's based on what you heard? Why did you even feel the need to tell me this?"

He shrugs. "You said Ronan was dating Vi."

I stumble over what all I want to say, because neither Ronan or Trevor are out, but I know they're both gay, so stumbling across two gay guys kissing would make sense, but by saying they're not out, I'm telling Kris that it's true.

Ronan and Trevor, though? Ronan wouldn't do that. And even if Trevor came out to him, I don't think they'd be making out in the basement. I just can't figure out why Kris would make this up. What does he get out of it?

"I don't want to deal with this right now," I say, glancing at my watch. "It's almost midnight."

"Why don't we just stay out here and enjoy the start of the new year together?" he asks, reaching for my wrist.

My brows furrow. "My friends and family are in there."

"I know, but I thought it would be nice if we had a romantic moment out here under the stars. Then we can go back to my place."

I snatch my arm back. "I don't know why you're assuming we're together again and everything's fine. You haven't even explained what happened or why you disappeared."

He blows into his hands before rubbing them together. "Look, I freaked out, okay? You said you loved me, and I panicked, thinking we were gonna start living together and planning a wedding."

"You can love someone without automatically planning a wedding. I thought we were happy. We had been together for a while, and I was just expressing to you how I felt."

"I know." He takes my hand. "I'm sorry. I can't justify the way I acted, but I feel bad. I heard you've been sleeping around, looking for someone who can fill my shoes, and I just—"

"What?" I yell. "What the hell are you talking about?"

He tilts his head, a smug grin on his face. "Word travels fast. You've been hooking up a lot lately, right? It's typical post break-up behavior. You're trying to lose yourself in other people so you don't think about me anymore. You're looking for me in every guy you come across. But nobody will be me, Renzo. I think we can start over and have a real chance."

"Wow," I say with a humorless chuckle. "You're really fucking full of yourself, aren't you?" I walk several steps away before spinning around to face him. "Do you actually believe I think about you when I fuck someone else?"

"I—"

I cut him off before he can get started. "So, you heard I've been having the time of my life, and you couldn't handle that, could you? You had to put a stop to it by coming back in my life and trying to tie yourself to me. You know, I knew you were a little possessive when we were dating. I thought you just loved me so much that you wanted me all to yourself. You wanted us to be locked in your place together, and I assumed it was because you enjoyed our time together that much. You were a little overprotective, but I thought it was because you cared. It turns out you're just a controlling asshole."

"Renzo stop," he says, his voice stern. "You don't know what you're talking about. Of course I cared. Of course I wanted to spend time with you, but I was..." He stops, pinning his lips together as his eyes flare with worry.

"What? What were you about to say? You might as well spit it out now."

He runs his hands through his hair, his frustration obvious. "I was going through some things."

"Like what?" I ask, annoyed.

"My ex had come back in the picture."

I laugh, not finding humor in this, but in absolute disbelief. I don't know what else to do, so I walk away before storming back. "You were with someone else at the same time? That's what you're saying?"

"Not the whole time."

I scoff. "That makes it better. You know what? I'm done. I don't even care anymore. You are far from who I thought you were."

"I didn't know what to do, okay?" he says. "I felt I owed him another chance, and when you told me you loved me, I thought about him and I knew I had to make a decision. I know now that it wasn't the right one, but I'm sorry. I fucked up."

"You know now? Why's that? He broke up with you?

Cheated on you? Up and left without a word? And now you hear that I'm doing just fine and you come barging in, acting like we can pick back up? I don't think so, Kris."

"And what? You're gonna go fuck that dude that's not even out? I'm the one who picked you up and put you back together after Luke hurt you. It's the same situation, do you not see that?"

I step up to him, my brows furrowed and my head cocked. "Who are you talking about?"

"Don't play stupid with me. I heard him talking about how y'all are messing around and how he likes you and all this shit."

"Wow, you're a piece of work." I step back. "You heard him say he liked me and you were quick to spin the story in your favor. You hoped I'd be mad at him. It was your last ditch attempt to pull me back to you." I shake my head as I walk backwards, away from him. "He's better than you in every way, and I'll wait as long as I have to for him to be ready to come out. I'm willing to do that for him, because I know he'd never treat me like you have."

"You say that now. I know you, Lorenzo. Don't forget that. You crave affection. You need it. You need to be publicly lauded, and it's all I ever did for you. You'll regret this."

Chapter Thirty-Three

I ONLY HAVE minutes to spare before midnight strikes, so I run into the house and find everyone congregating in the living room getting ready to watch the ball drop on TV.

"There you are!"

"Hurry up!"

"Where've you been?"

"It's about time."

The chorus of annoyance slams into me as I approach everyone.

"Sorry, sorry. I'm here."

Ronan angles his body slightly to get a look at me, and all I want to do is hold his face in my hands and kiss him passionately, but I can't, so I give him a wink and crooked grin.

Vi passes me a confetti popper and noise maker. "Where's Kris?"

I shrug. "Gone, I guess. Doesn't matter."

I don't miss the sly grin that grows on her face as her eyes flicker to Ronan.

"Ten, nine, eight..." Mom and Dad chant the countdown and everyone else joins in, their eyes focused on the TV.

"Three, two, one. Happy New Year!" everyone yells, blowing the noise makers and popping confetti into the air.

Behind the safety of the couch, I reach out and squeeze Ronan's fingers. "Happy New Year."

When he looks at me, he grins. "Happy New Year."

Everybody begins to embrace each other, starting with my parents, Vi and her friends, and then they hug my friends. I jump at the opportunity to wrap my arms around Ronan.

"Thank you for being here," I whisper in his ear.

"Of course," he replies.

As much as I don't want to, I pull away and make my way to my friends to embrace them and everyone else, and Vi passes me up to give Ronan a hug.

After several minutes, Mom taps on her wine glass with a spoon. "As always, we love having you all here. There's nothing better than holidays spent with family and friends, all of us surrounded by love and friendship."

Once done with her short speech, she calls me and Vi over.

"What's up?" Vi asks.

"Me and your father are going to go up and pack, then we'll be heading to a hotel near the airport, because our flight leaves early. Your friends can stay over as long as you promise to be responsible. I'd rather you be here than go out, because there will be drunk drivers out there and at least I'll know you're all safe."

"Yes, ma'am," I reply.

"Suck up," Vi mumbles.

"No funny business," Mom continues, staring at Vi. "I expect you know what I'm talking about."

"Why is it always me?" Vi cries. "Why doesn't Zo get the *no funny business* talk?"

"Lorenzo doesn't have a boyfriend here, does he?"

Vi pins her lips together, her body tense. I really owe her for this.

My dad wraps his arm around my mom's shoulders and gives me a look I can't decipher.

"I just don't want you to get pregnant, sweetie. We've talked about this before. Your father and I aren't stupid. We know you two are growing up, and you'll likely start making adult decisions."

"Mom, it's okay. Vi's really responsible. She's smarter than me, probably," I say, resting my arm on Vi's shoulder. "We remember the sex talk. Abstinence is key, but if you must unlock that door, condoms are essential," I say, repeating the line she's fed us since we were twelve.

"Okay, it's really weird to have this talk with our friends ten feet away," Vi says.

Dad laughs. "We'll leave you alone now."

"But I—" Mom starts.

"Honey, it's really okay. Trust me," Dad says, escorting Mom away. "Condoms. Both of you," Dad says, staring at me.

I cut my gaze at Vi, who looks just as confused.

"That was weird. Why did Dad look at you like that?" Vi asks.

"Who knows, but at least we have the house to ourselves again."

"You just want to do perverted things to Ronan."

"With Ronan, but yes."

She rolls her eyes and laughs. "Anyway, you're gonna have to explain some things to him first. Like what the hell was going on with you and Kris tonight."

"I know, I know."

We make our way back to our friends and wait for our parents to leave before we break out some of the alcohol and really start to celebrate the new year.

~

It's a little after two in the morning when Jayden passes out on the couch in the basement, and Scarlet goes up to Vi's room to sleep. Monique, Vi, Trevor, and Dex are all playing some weird game that Vi swears is real but I'm pretty sure she just made it up.

"Okay, if you roll a seven, you have to tell us a secret nobody knows. If you roll a twelve, you have to drink whatever I pour in this glass."

"What? Hell no," Dex says.

"Just do it!"

I laugh, shaking my head. "She's definitely making this up as she goes," I tell Ronan.

"Seems like it."

"Wanna come upstairs with me real quick?"

His head snaps in my direction. "What?"

"Nobody's paying attention. I'll leave first and I'll wait for you at the top of the stairs."

His eyes glance around the room. "Are you sure?"

"That I want to be alone with you? Yes, I'm dying."

Ronan's cheeks tinge pink as he smiles. "Okay, go."

I end up waiting for almost ten minutes before I see him round the corner and start jogging up the stairs. My smile grows the closer he gets.

Once he hits the second floor, I grab his hand and pull him to my room, close and lock the door, and then press him up against it.

"I've been dying to kiss you."

"So do it."

With my hand on the back of his neck, I slam my mouth against his. It's not a soft, romantic kiss. It's needy and desperate, because that's how I feel right now.

He moans as my tongue dips into his mouth, and his hands find a place on my back as I groan, the sound rumbling in my chest.

"I've missed your mouth," I say, before diving back in and licking the seam of his lips before he allows me in again.

We're frenzied and breathing heavily before long, and all I want to do is rip his clothes off and toss him into my bed, but I want to get a few things off my chest first, so I manage to pull myself away from him.

"That's what I wanted to do at midnight."

He chuckles. "Not sure everyone else would've enjoyed that."

"Come here," I say, bringing him to my bed. I turn on the lamp on my nightstand and sit on the edge of the mattress. "First of all, I want to apologize for tonight. It didn't go as I planned, and Kris's appearance was unexpected. I'm sorry I was preoccupied with him most of the night, but I want you to know I never considered getting back with him. He has this way about him that kind of traps you in place. I can't explain it, but know that at the end of the night, I ended things once and for all. He's not a good person, and while it sucks that I didn't see it earlier, I'm glad I know I dodged a bullet. He tried lying to me about you and Trevor hooking up because he overheard a conversation you two were having, and I realized he was attempting to turn me off from you."

"Wait, what?" His brows furrow and this is the first time I think I've ever seen him angry. His jaw is clenched and his nostrils flare as he breathes. "He said I was hooking up with Trevor?"

I touch his knee, hoping to calm him. "I didn't believe it for a second."

He takes a breath and tilts his head up, his eyes focused on the ceiling. When he meets my gaze again, he says, "I told Trevor. We were talking about you and Kris, and anyway, I told him I liked you. He asked to talk downstairs, and he ended up coming out to me. We were only talking."

I give him a reassuring grin. "I believe you. But hey, I'm glad you and Trevor can talk now."

"Yeah, we talked about how much of a whorebag you are."

I throw my head back and laugh. "Of course."

Ronan chuckles for a few seconds before saying, "Oh, and I think your dad knows about us."

Chapter Thirty-Four

"I'M SORRY. WHAT?" My eyes nearly pop out of my head.

"Yeah, I don't know. We had this weird conversation outside earlier. I went out to get some air and saw you and Kris talking. A little bit later, your dad comes out, sees you two, and then starts talking about how he's known as this quiet guy, but how he's always aware of what's going on." He waves his hand through the air. "Anyway, he tells me to take a good look and realize some things aren't as they seem. It was like he knew I was upset but was telling me if I paid close enough attention I could see that you two were arguing rather than...reacquainting. Then he said something like he might not know how things got the way they are, but that it was obvious what was going on, because Violet isn't acting like she's into me, but that you seemed to be very happy up at the cabin and stuff."

"Wow. I can't say I'm too surprised. The man does always seem to know what's going on, and that explains the weird look he gave me earlier. But how do you feel?"

He looks down at the comforter, rubbing his hands across

his pants before he stares into my eyes. "I feel like I need to explain to them what's going on. I mean, I felt relieved that he didn't seem to be judging me, but I want them to know I'm not doing anything behind Vi's back. I don't know. I guess we can tell them the truth now. I just wish it would be as easy to tell my parents."

I run my hand up his thigh. "I know. It'll be okay, let's not worry about this right now. I want us to be able to exchange our presents."

Ronan gives me a bashful smile. "I only brought one. You may have one already, but—"

"Give it to me already," I say, holding my hand out. Ronan stands up and slips his hand in his pocket. "You about to propose to me?"

He smirks. "Not quite."

When I grab the foiled square from his hand, my eyebrows shoot up. "What...is this? Are you saying?"

"Yep."

I yank on his arm, tugging him to the bed. "Then we can worry about the rest later. You win. Best present ever."

I get him on his back, and I crawl over him, making sure I kiss him slowly. I want nothing more than to ravage him. I've wanted this moment since I first laid eyes on his handsome face, but now that I know him...now that I like him...I want this to be special. I want him to forever look back on this and enjoy the memory.

"I'm not gonna be able to top this," I whisper into his neck as I grind against him.

"I know I'm new at this, but I'm pretty sure you're about to top me right now."

I chuckle and gently bite a section of flesh below his ear. "I meant this gift."

"Well, if you top me well enough, I'd say that would be a pretty good present."

I hover above him and grin. "Oh, it's gonna be better than *well enough.*"

He smiles and yanks me down until our mouths meet again. I pull away to rip my shirt over my head and toss it to the floor, and he does the same.

Leaning over him again, I plant soft kisses across his chest, swiping his nipple with my tongue before traveling lower. My hands begin to undo his pants while my mouth explores the dips and curves of his abs.

Ronan raises his hips so I can pull the material down his legs, leaving him completely exposed. I get off the bed just to remove the rest of my clothes and grab the lube from the nightstand, then I take my place between his legs again.

I take him in my mouth, stroking his shaft while teasing his crown with my tongue. His hands fly to my head, his fingers tangling in my hair.

"Fuck, Renzo," he breathes.

I take him to the back of my throat, enjoying the sounds of pleasure that fall from his lips. I bring him to the edge of an orgasm before I back away and reach for the lube.

"You ready?"

He nods. "I've been trying some things."

"Oh yeah?" I ask, arching a brow. "I'm gonna need to watch you *try things*, because I'm intrigued."

Ronan cracks a grin. "I didn't want to be completely caught off guard, but I didn't mess with anything nearly as big as your dick, so..."

I squirt the lube onto my fingers and rub them against his hole. "I won't hurt you, and if it's too much, let me know."

He throws his head back deeper into the pillow while squeezing his eyes shut. "Okay. Yeah."

I suck his cock back into my mouth while my fingers slowly prod at his entrance. I dip the tip of my finger inside, testing the waters. He clenches immediately.

Pulling off his cock, I run my other hand over his stomach. "Breathe and relax."

He nods again, taking a deep breath, so I try again. I get to the first knuckle before I start rotating my finger a little. I stroke him with my left hand while I continue the slow journey of my finger into his ass. Once my finger is all the way in, he exhales.

"Keep breathing, baby. Try to relax. It'll feel good soon."

Carefully, and at a snail's pace, I move my finger in and out, starting with small increments. His breathing becomes ragged and when he reaches for his cock, I smile.

"More?"

It takes several minutes, but I enjoy every second of the time spent getting Ronan ready for my cock. Once he's comfortable with two fingers, and after he's begged me for more, I remove my digits and quickly grab a condom to roll over my length. After another squirt of lube, I spread his legs apart and climb between them.

"You sure?" I ask again, my cock in hand while the tip rests against the tight hole.

"Just do it already," he pants.

I chuckle. "So bossy for a virgin."

I gently guide myself in, watching him closely.

"Fuck," he breathes.

"Okay?"

"Yeah," he grunts, squeezing the covers.

I push in a little further and he clenches around me. "Oh shit," I exclaim.

As I get deeper inside, I brace myself over him, and his hands go to my biceps, squeezing the muscles as I sink into his ass.

Fully seated, I brush hair from his forehead and kiss him. "Good?"

Ronan bites his lip and rotates his hips, causing both of us to moan.

"Yeah, I'm good."

I start rocking back and forth, moving in and out, and watch as his face flushes red. His eyes meet mine, and he's completely blissed out. His teeth sink into his bottom lip while he watches me move, and I quickly determine I'll never want to be anywhere else but here.

"You feel so good," I breathe.

"Mmm," he moans, closing his eyes and pressing his fingers into my back.

I back up and hold his knees in my hands while I watch my cock move in and out of his tight warmth. "Fucking Christ, Ronan. You're perfect."

He whimpers, reaching for his cock. "You're so good," he says.

I pick up the pace a little, and when he doesn't protest, but instead strokes himself faster, I keep it up, diving deeper into his ass.

His muscles flex as he jerks his cock, and it's the most beautiful sight I've ever seen. Ronan is fucking beautiful. From his pouty lips and high cheekbones to his muscled arms and abs, and the most perfect looking cock I've ever seen. Seeing him laid out like this is doing things to me. Not just bringing me closer to an explosive orgasm, but other things...deeper things. I tell myself it's just the moment. It's only because I'm fucking him that I'm thinking this way, but I'm not sure. I think I might love him.

"Oh shit," he cries.

His cum shoots out and lands on his stomach, and it sends me over the edge. I grip his hips and pummel into him until I'm coming several seconds later.

"Fuck!"

Ronan

Chapter Thirty-Five

SHORTLY AFTER RENZO pulls out and tosses the condom in the trash, he hands me a tissue and collapses next to me. "You're perfect."

I laugh him off, wiping the cum from my stomach. "You're just high off endorphins."

"I do feel a little high," he says, nuzzling into my arm. "Your ass is like the best drug."

"Well, your cock is pretty okay too."

He playfully pinches my side. "Don't hurt my ego."

I turn to my side slowly and study him. His eyes are closed and his face is relaxed. I have no doubt he'll be asleep soon.

"I say this with no hesitation. You're the best I've ever had."

His eyes snap open and I grin. "You're a smartass, you know that?"

I laugh. "I'm kidding. Well, I'm not, but I'm sure you're better than everyone else in the world."

"I hope..." He starts, clamps his lips together, and decides to continue. "I hope you never find out otherwise."

It takes a few seconds before I understand his meaning. I lean in and kiss him softly. "I'm only interested in you."

"But I'm the only person...the first person that you..."

I stop him by putting my finger on his lips. "Why would I want anyone else when I have you?"

He gives me a partial grin, like he doesn't believe me. I don't understand how Lorenzo Hayes, the rich, popular, charming guy who can have anyone, would have any insecurities. How is he worried about me wanting anyone else when it's me who should be worried?

"I'm gonna go clean up," I say, kissing his forehead. "I'll be back."

"Hurry."

I laugh as I gingerly get off the bed and head to the bathroom. I'm glad he's half asleep, otherwise he'd be making fun of the way I'm walking.

Once I'm done in the bathroom, I crawl back into his bed, and he quickly makes me the little spoon as he wraps his long arm around my waist and pulls me into him.

His breathing evens out, and I know he's fast asleep, but my thoughts keep me awake.

Renzo's amazing. He's funny and caring. He loves his friends and his family in a way I've never seen. He's confident and charming, and he's so fucking hot I can barely believe I'm with him. But I feel like we aren't really together. How can I call him mine when only a few people know about us?

Everyone is right. He doesn't deserve to be hidden. He's the best person I know, and it's wrong of me to have him change who he is in order to be with me. We shouldn't only have stolen moments behind closed doors. I want us to be like any other couple, but I'm having a hard time figuring out how to unlock and open that closet door.

~

As much as I hated doing it, I left Renzo in his bed and fled his house before anybody was awake. I sent him a text that he'll see as soon as he checks his phone, and I hope he won't be too mad, but I don't have much time. I have to visit my parents and be back before school starts up again. Plus, I felt if I waited any longer, I wouldn't do it.

So after stopping at my dorm and grabbing some things, I hopped back in the car and started the almost twelve hour drive to New Hampshire.

I had plenty of moments where I almost talked myself out of it and turned the car back around. I'm not excited to tell my parents, but it's a necessary step. I have to get it out. I have to come out to them before I can breathe a little easier.

I don't bother calling ahead. I'm sure they'll be home. I go over every possible scenario I think could happen and try to plan how I'll react or what I'll say, but I know in the moment everything will change.

Renzo calls me five hours into my trip. His voice is scratchy and I can tell he just woke up.

"What're you doing?" he asks.

"I have to take care of something."

"Are you running away from me?" He asks in a joking manner, but I can hear the worry in his tone.

"No, of course not."

He takes a breath. "So, you're coming back?"

I chuckle. "I'm coming back. I do have to finish college."

"Fuck college, I'm here."

"You're saying you're more important than education?" I tease.

"Well...yeah."

I laugh, missing him already. "I have to do this now."

"I think I know what you're doing. I would've loved to have been there for you, but I understand. Good luck, but remember if it doesn't go the way you hope, you have me,

Violet, and my parents, and some friends that will accept you with open arms. You have people who lo...who care."

My heart nearly explodes and I know without a doubt that there is no going back. I have to tell my parents, and whether they accept me or not, they have to know I found someone. They have to know who I am. And even if I go back to Michigan without their support, I know I'm going to end up in the arms of someone who makes me feel happier than I ever have.

Chapter Thirty-Six

THE DRIVE through Sugar Hill brings back a plethora of memories. I had a decent childhood living here. Not the best, but definitely not the worst. I never really felt like I fit in, but I had a couple close friends growing up. After high school, we all lost contact with each other. I think each of us were dying to get away from this sleepy town and didn't want any ties to the place in which none of us felt we belonged.

I sometimes think about Jonah and Alexis and hope they're happier wherever they are now.

When I drive up toward my parents' house, my heart jumps into my throat, beating at a rapid pace. It's now or never. It's just past eight o'clock when I park in the driveway, to the right of the basketball goal I spent a lot of time using.

There's a couple warm lights on downstairs—one in the living room and the other in the kitchen, letting me know they're awake. I'd take bets that Dad is sitting in his recliner, watching TV, and Mom's probably preparing food for tomorrow's lunch.

I exit my car and pull my coat around me, heading to the

front door. With one last deep breath, I press the doorbell and wait.

Mom answers, wearing an apple covered apron. Her confusion switches to surprise and finally a smile.

"Ronan, oh my goodness, get in here."

I step inside and she closes the door before she wraps her arms around me.

"Hey, Mom."

"Let me look at you. Are you okay? Why are you here? And at this hour?"

She rests her hands in her pockets as she stands in the doorway that leads from the mudroom to the living room.

"I'm okay. How are you?"

"I was just saving some leftovers for lunch tomorrow. Did your father know you were coming? Let's go inside."

I spot Dad in his chair, and his thick eyebrows shoot up. "What's going on?"

"Just thought I'd come for a quick visit before school starts back up."

"Well, it's a good thing we were actually here. It's not the best idea to surprise someone with a visit."

"Keith, stop," Mom chides quietly.

"It's okay," I say. "I'm sorry. I know, but I guess I just hoped for the best."

"Come in, sit down," Mom says, ushering me to the couch. "You hungry?"

"I am, actually."

"I'll bring you something."

She flutters off, leaving me and my dad sitting in silence as we both stare at the TV. I suddenly feel like I was transported back in time several years, and I'm a child again, afraid of saying the wrong thing.

"So, how was your Christmas?"

"Typical. We saw your Aunt Emma and Uncle Jack this year. They asked about you."

He said it in a way that's supposed to make me feel bad for not going. "Oh. Well, I'm okay. I spent the holiday with some friends."

"Christmas is time for family, not friends," he grunts, not looking at me.

Mom comes back just in time. "I'm glad you weren't alone on Christmas. Who are these friends? Are they good people?"

"Yes, ma'am. They're really great."

I take the plate from her and dive into the leftovers of what was probably their dinner earlier—pot roast and rolls.

"Is there still some left for tomorrow?" Dad gripes.

"Yes, there's plenty," she says, taking a seat next to me. "So what brings you out here?"

I hesitate. Dad doesn't seem like he's in a good mood, but honestly, this seemed to be his typical demeanor when I was around before, so I'm not sure he gets happier than this. The man is chronically upset. I think he likes to find something to be angry about.

"Just coming for a visit," I say, forcing a smile.

"That's bullshit," Dad says, standing up.

"Keith!" Mom cries.

"What? He up and left right after graduating and hasn't been back since. He hardly calls, so we don't know what the hell he's up to most of the time, and now he's here for a visit? Something is going on."

I place my plate on the brown coffee table and stand up. "Do you ever wonder why I don't call or visit? Has it ever crossed your mind that it's because I never felt like you cared about me? Don't pretend we had some amazing relationship."

"You had a roof over your head, food on your plate, and

everything you could ever want," Dad says, pointing his finger at me.

"Not everything," I say.

"What?" he seethes, running a hand over his beard. "Don't you dare be ungrateful."

"You're thinking materialistically. I know I had a lot, but all I wanted was to feel like I could actually talk to you and have you listen. I wanted to feel loved and accepted, instead you did everything you could to make me feel like I was an unwanted presence in your life. Like I was a mistake."

"You were!" he snaps.

Mom gasps behind me. "Keith, stop it. Stop it right now."

"No, he wants to come into my house and spout this shit about feelings and emotions, well he's gonna hear how I feel. You were a mistake. We didn't think your mom could get pregnant, but here you are. I never planned on having kids, but I did what I needed to make sure you survived."

"Stop it!" Mom cries. "He was a miracle. He was what God wanted for us."

"Oh!" Dad makes a noise while cutting the air with his hand, like he doesn't believe that.

Being a surprise baby isn't all that shocking, to be honest. It happens to a lot of people, but the fact that he said I was a mistake instead of an accident or a surprise definitely cuts a little deeper. Everything makes sense now. He never made any attempts to be close to me, and I guess it's because he never wanted me in the first place.

"Ronan," Mom says, grabbing me by the arms and turning me to face her. "You were wanted. You were loved. I love you now. You have to believe that."

I nod, appreciating that at least one parent seems to care, but once I tell them I'm gay, I wonder if her feelings will change. Mom was always the more loving of the two, but I think she fell in line with a lot of what Dad wanted and didn't do any more than he'd be okay with.

Mom rushes off, heading down the dark hall, sniffling, and before I can fully spin around, Dad is in my space, grabbing my jacket.

"If you think you're gonna come in here and tell your mother that you're some fruitcake, you've got another thing coming, because I won't allow that to happen," he growls, spitting on my face as he speaks.

"Wha-what are you talking about?" I stammer, wondering how he could possibly know.

He sneers, loving the fear wafting off of me. "I found one of your pervert magazines. Think I didn't know? Oh, I know. I've known for a while. No son of mine will parade around with another man, thinking it's okay."

I forgot I got one of those magazines years ago at my friend's cousin's house. I found it while we were going through boxes in his garage, looking for a photo album his mom wanted. On top of being unwanted, this would explain his absolute disdain for me. "You don't want me anyway."

"You can go do your pride festivals wherever the hell you live, but you will not bring that shit here. I will not be known in this town as the man who raised a faggot."

The slur slaps me across the face, and I jolt back, my jaw dropping. Tears burn the backs of my eyes, because while I'm aware of the word, and thought about how it could be hurled at me, I never imagined I'd hear it with such hatred coming from the mouth of one of my parents.

When I hear a whimper, I look over and find my mom standing in the doorway, a tissue in hand, covering her mouth.

"Mom." My voice breaks as I call for her. In this moment I've never felt like I needed her more. I need her to have my back. To be on my side. To understand.

"Get out!" Dad yells, pointing at the door. "Get out of my

house. How dare you come here to upset your mother like this."

My eyes bounce from my dad to my mom, hoping she steps in and stops him, but she's never stood up to my dad, so I shouldn't expect her to now.

"Mom," I say again, turning to move in her direction.

Her eyes are as wet as mine, tears falling down both of our cheeks, but she's stuck in place as she stares at me like she isn't sure who she's looking at anymore.

"I said get out!" Dad says, yanking me back by my jacket. "We're done here."

I stumble backwards and then slowly make my way to the door as I plead with my mom via my eyes, begging her to run to me and say it's okay.

She brings her hand down and looks like she's about to say something, but she doesn't. She watches me walk out into the cold.

Chapter Thirty-Seven

I'M IN MY CAR, bawling like a baby, unsure of where to go or what to do now. I have some money in my account, so I can try to find a room to stay in, but this didn't go at all like I had imagined in the fifteen different scenarios I played out.

Dad already knew. That was a surprise I wasn't expecting. I figured I'd get some preachy lecture about God and the Bible and what's wrong and right, but I didn't expect blatant hate and disgust and slurs. I didn't expect my mom to look at me like a stranger. I didn't expect her silence.

After about ten minutes, I wipe my eyes and begin backing out of the long driveway. When I'm near the street, I spot my mom bursting through the front door, frantically waving her arms.

I slam on the brakes and shift into drive to get closer. Dad appears in the doorway, yelling something.

Mom gets in the passenger seat, tears covering her cheeks. "Let's go to a hotel. We'll talk there."

I don't question her. I don't say a single word on the way into town and toward the first hotel I find. She doesn't say anything either. I only hear her sniffling as she stares out the window, but her fleeing the house to join me has to be a good sign.

When I pull into a parking spot, she gets out without a word and heads for the lobby. She may not be as upset as Dad, but she doesn't seem too thrilled either. I guess I shouldn't be surprised.

With a deep breath, I shut off the car and follow her inside. She spins away from the counter when I approach, holding a key in her hand.

"Second floor," she says simply, her eyes red and puffy.

The clerk eyes me strangely, probably confused about our predicament.

Once in the room, I take a quick glance around and notice the dark green carpet with gold swirls to match the golden comforters on each of the twin size beds.

Mom disappears into the bathroom to the left and I plop onto the bed nearest the door so she can be closer to the heater near the window.

A few minutes later, she emerges and removes her coat and apron and lays them carefully across her bed. When she sits and faces me, my pulse picks up speed.

"What your father..." she stumbles over the words, her voice shaky, so she begins again. "What your father said. That was wrong."

"But I am—"

She raises her hand, cutting me off. "You're gay." She nods once and swallows. "There was no need for him to use that slur."

At the revelation that she has my back and that she doesn't feel the same way he does, I drop my head in my hands and cry, my shoulders shaking with each sob.

The bed dips to my right and her arms snake around me,

pulling me into her, and I cry even harder. I cry like I've never cried before. It's overwhelming.

Mom sniffles and sobs along with me. When I finally pull myself together, she scoots back a little, but holds onto my hands.

"Talk to me," she says.

I shake my head, unsure of where to start. With a small shrug, I say, "I think I'm in love."

Mom's face emits two different things at the same time, sadness and joy. How it's possible, I don't know. Her lips pull up into a partial smile, but her eyes are sad, and she sheds a few more tears. She attempts to talk, but the words never come.

"I've been gay my whole life, Mom. It's not a choice I made; it's who I am. I've heard you and Dad talk before. I've heard enough to know how you both feel about it, so I hid that part of myself, but I can't change."

Mom reaches to the nightstand separating the beds and pulls a Kleenex from the box. She dabs her cheeks and nose. "Ronan, we...I mean, I don't know what to say. We raised you in church."

I shake my head. "That doesn't change anything. All that means is that I've been told since I was a child that I'd go to hell for being who I am. I've been afraid nearly my whole life."

Her hand flies to her chest like her heart hurts. "That's never what I intended. My father was a pastor, you know that, and I know we're a little old school with a lot of things, but even I was taught it was a sin. Your father was raised the same way."

I shake my head, not wanting to have a discussion about religion. That's not what this is about. "I wanted to let you know, because I met someone and I've never been happier. I came here to get it off my chest so I could start living my life out loud. I don't have much hope for Dad considering all that he said, but I hope you can accept this, Mom. I'd hate to lose both parents."

She sobs again, gripping my hand tighter. "I love you. You are my son, and you will always be my son. This may take some time to wrap my head around, but you'll never lose me. I don't agree with your father on a lot of things, and this is one of them. You were not a mistake, do you hear me?" she says, grabbing my chin. "You were meant to be my child, and I'm sorry if I ever made you feel like you couldn't be yourself. Your father has a dominant personality, and it's usually easier to stay quiet in order for things to run smoother, but that won't happen anymore."

I bring her in for a hug and whisper, "Thank you."

When we separate, she wipes her tears again and exhales. "So, you're in love?"

I duck my head. "I think so."

"Tell me about him."

And I do. I leave out any details that may make her uncomfortable, but I explain how he makes me feel, and how he treats me, and how he's willing to keep us a secret since I'm not out.

"He sounds selfless. There's not many people like that, and it sounds like he really cares about you. I'm glad you're happy," she says with a small smile.

"Thanks for giving me a chance. What's gonna happen with you and Dad?"

"I don't know. I can't believe some of the stuff that came out of his mouth tonight. We're going to have to have a long talk, but not tonight, and maybe not tomorrow. I'll stay here until I feel like going back home and dealing with him. He needs time to cool down and think about what it's going to be like to lose his family."

My eyes widen at the implication. "Mom."

She pats my arm. "Don't worry."

We spend the rest of the night talking about how school's going and how I like Michigan. We don't speak about Dad again, and we don't talk about my being gay, we just catch up, and it feels nice.

Renzo

Chapter Thirty-Eight

RONAN ENDED up staying in New Hampshire for a few extra days, dealing with some family issues. We've talked on the phone, so I'm aware of how his parents handled the news, and while it wasn't the best, it could've been worse, and I'm happy his mom is on his side.

He hasn't given me all the details yet, but it seems like things between his parents aren't that great right now, and he doesn't want to leave his mom yet.

I haven't heard from him since early yesterday morning, but today is the first day back to school, so I'm thinking he'll be back soon.

"Everything okay with him?" Vi asks as I drive her to school.

"I think so. He feels bad leaving her in a hotel when she left the house for him. Seems to have caused a rift between his parents. Mom is choosing to love her son and the dad doesn't want anything to do with him."

"That's sad," Vi says, looking down at her lap. "Parents are supposed to love their children unconditionally."

"Sadly, there are conditions for a lot of parents."

I drop her off in front of the highschool. "Have a good first day back."

"You too. Thanks for driving me. I swear my car hates me."

"I think you hate your car."

"How was I supposed to see whatever it was that made a huge hole in my tire?"

I chuckle. "See ya later."

Vi's constantly getting flat tires, bumping into things, or getting it taken away for some reason or another. Luckily, the college isn't too far away from her school.

I check my phone again before I start driving, but I still haven't heard from Ronan. I try not to be disappointed, because I know he's going through a lot right now, but I just miss him so damn much.

On campus, I find Jayden, Trevor, Dex, and a few other people lingering outside one of the buildings.

"Can't wait to never come back to this place," I say in lieu of a greeting.

"I know. How dare we get an education," Jayden jokes.

"Not everyone loves school as much as you," Dex tells him. "You're always the teacher's pet."

Jayden grins but doesn't say anything.

"So what's up with Ronan?" Dex asks me while everyone continues talking about other things.

"Not sure. I'll call him later."

"But he told them? Does that mean he'll tell people here?"

I shrug. "I don't know."

"Guess I should get to class," Jayden says.

"Me too," Trevor adds. "I gotta get across campus."

Before I turn to walk away, I spot a familiar face round the building.

Ronan.

My eyebrows shoot up and a huge smile takes over my

face. I want to rush toward him and wrap him in a hug and tell him I missed him. I know it's only been a week, but I guess that in itself speaks volumes.

"Oh hey," Dex says, lifting his chin to greet him.

I shove my hands deeper into the pockets of my jacket, trying to control my excitement. He grins at me, looking damn good in his typical preppy attire. He's wearing black jeans, a cream-colored cable knit sweater with an open tweed jacket and scarf. God I love looking at him.

He gets closer, greets the guys, then steps right up to me and grins. "Hey, handsome."

Shock blankets my face, but then I give him a crooked smile. "Hey, yourself."

Ronan circles my wrist, tugs me into him and plants a kiss on my mouth. I stiffen for just the briefest of seconds before I reciprocate. It's a quick kiss, but it means the world to me.

"Umm."

"What is happening?"

"Uhh. Confused."

Just a few things I hear my friends say, but I focus on Ronan. "Yeah?"

He knows what I mean and nods once, taking my hand in his. "Yeah."

I put my lips near his ear. "Are you trying to make me fall in love with you?" It's a joke. My normal teasing nature coming out to make light of a pretty big situation, but his response shuts me up.

"Maybe. It would only be fair."

As I stare at him in wonderment and disbelief, Jayden's voice breaks through my thoughts.

"Fuckin' Renzo, man. Why am I even surprised?" He laughs. "This dude gets anyone he wants." He puts his arm around some girl. "Even his sister's boyfriend. We'll talk later," he calls out, walking away.

"So, it's official now," Dex says, clapping me on the back. "Congrats you two."

Trevor gives us both a small smile and a nod. We're the only ones who know about him, but maybe this will give him some courage to come out himself.

After everyone scatters off, I squeeze Ronan's hand. "Fuck, I've missed you."

"I've missed you too."

"So, you're out."

"I'm out." He smiles and my heart skips a beat.

I let go of his hand and drape my arm around his shoulders and kiss his temple. "And you're mine. Please tell me you'll come to my place tonight, because we have some things to do."

He laughs. "Oh yeah? What kind of things?"

"Dirty, nasty, filthy things. You'll love it."

Epilogue

IT'S APRIL FOURTEENTH, which means it's my twenty-first birthday. Since not all of my friends are twenty-one yet, there will be no club-hopping or anything like that, but we are all getting together at my new apartment.

I figured the best way to celebrate being twenty-one was finally having my own place. Not gonna lie, I didn't hate living with my parents. Maybe that's weird, but it's not like they had strict rules with me, and like I said before, they go out of town a lot, but Vi is eighteen now, and perfectly capable of being on her own when they leave. Not that she wasn't when she was seventeen, but my parents tend to treat her like she's a fragile doll. She now uses the *I'm an adult* line quite a bit.

It's only been about five months since Ronan's been in my life, but I can't imagine not having him around. I floated the idea of him moving in with me, but he waved me off like I was joking, but I'm not. Since I moved in a few weeks ago, he's spent nearly all his time here anyway. My place is close to campus, so it works for both of us.

I get that it's early in our relationship for living together, but when you know, you know, and this feels right. I can't imagine anything he'd do to make me want to end things. However, he might be hesitant because I've yet to say I love him. I know, I know, but he hasn't said it either.

In January, when he showed up on campus and came out to all my close friends by kissing me, and mentioned something about maybe, possibly being in love, by saying it'd only be fair if I fell for him, he's said nothing since.

I chalked it up to misunderstanding. Maybe he was excited about coming out and caught up in the moment. Not to mention, I've been wary of saying those three little words again since the last time didn't end up too well for me.

However, it's not fair for me to take that situation out on him by not expressing my feelings. I do love Ronan. I probably fell in love at the cabin if I'm being honest, and it's time to tell him.

My mom's been telling me it's obvious I'm in love ever since she found out we were actually together. That conversation was interesting to say the least. Like Ronan told me, Dad knew, but Mom was caught off guard.

Me, Ronan, and Violet all sat down at the dining room table with my parents one night and came clean. Mom tried to show her disappointment in us for lying, but she was too giddy about my new relationship that she hardly did more than purse her lips and shake her head.

She apologized to Vi for acting the way she did about her and Ronan when it was actually me and Ronan who were doing the *funny business*.

Once she was certain that Vi was okay with what happened and realized they were never serious, she easily accepted the new dynamic. Dad mostly nodded and grinned, smug that he had figured it out before anyone told him, but he was happy to finally have the details on how everything happened.

As I'm walking down the hall and into my living room, I see Ronan come up the steps of the porch. He knocks on the screen door and smiles when he sees me.

I wave him in. "How many times have I told you you don't have to knock?"

"I don't know. Sixteen?"

"When are you gonna listen?"

"I don't know. Never?"

I shake my head and pull him into me, planting a kiss on his soft lips. When I pull away, I grab his hand and bring him to the kitchen with me. "Hungry?"

"I could eat. When are people coming over?" he asks.

"Not for a while. Probably a few hours."

"Oh okay."

I grab leftovers of the spaghetti I made last night and pop them in the microwave. "You talk to your mom?"

"Yeah, she says hi," he replies with a grin.

I haven't met his mom yet, which isn't too abnormal considering she doesn't live in the state, but I have actually had a conversation with her over FaceTime when she called Ronan.

She tried to make it work with her husband, but it became too much when Ronan's dad continued to use slurs and had nothing but hateful things to say about their son and the way he *chooses* to live his life. So now she's in the process of moving to her own place, and has invited us to come visit in the summer when she's settled.

After we eat, and as I'm putting the dishes in the dishwasher, Ronan leaves to get my present out of his car.

When he returns, he drops a bag on the counter and smiles. "You can't open it until later."

"Is it another condom? Because now that we've been able to have sex without them, I don't really want to go back."

He laughs. "No, it's not a condom."

I grab him by the hand and bring him to the couch. "Good, but I have something I want to talk to you about."

"I really hope you're not gonna break-up with me, because that will make the gift a little awkward."

I chuckle. "No, I'm not breaking up with you. Are you crazy? You're stuck with me. It's almost like you don't even have a choice."

"Are you kidnapping me?" His eyes twinkle with humor

I tilt my head and pretend to really think about it. "I might."

He laughs and rolls his eyes. "God, I love you."

Both of us freeze and the laughter fades as we stare at each other. He clearly didn't mean to say it. It just rolled off his tongue like any other statement.

"What?"

He licks his lips and sits forward, taking my hand in his. "I love you, Renzo. There's nothing not to love, and I wanted to say it sooner, but I wasn't sure how you'd react because it was so early. However, it's become work to keep from saying it," he says with a laugh. "So often you do or say things that make me want to say it. And you deserve to know you're loved. So, yeah," he finishes awkwardly.

My heart skips a beat and a warm feeling explodes in my chest. I've never heard those words from anyone I've ever been with, and hearing them come from Ronan's mouth makes me glad he's the first.

"I...uhh." I run my hand through my hair. "I'm kinda mad you stole my thunder, to be honest, because I brought you over here to this couch so I could finally tell you that I'm in love with you and that I have been since the cabin, and that I was afraid to crack my heart open and spill my feelings, but that you needed to know how much you mean to me."

A chuckle breaks through his lips. "Uhh. I'm sorry?"

I shake my head, playfully rolling my eyes while I crack a

smile. "I love you." The words feel so good leaving my tongue, but I know it's because of who they're going to.

"I love you," he repeats, blushing.

I reach out and cradle the back of his head and bring him in for a passionate kiss. My tongue pushes past his lips and entwines with his.

I ease away and look him straight in the eye. "Oh, and I want you to move in with me."

May 22nd. The day Ronan finally moved in with me. He waited until the end of the school year, and we moved all his shit to our place in two trips.

Everyone talks about how living together can cause problems in a relationship, because there's no getting away from that person, but so far it's been perfect, and I don't want to be away from him anyway. He stayed over so often, it's hardly different than when he wasn't living here.

"Summer break, what's the plan?" Dex asks, making himself at home while reaching into the fridge to get a soda.

"Well, we both work, but we do have plans to visit his mom in the next month or so, and besides that, we'll probably spend most of our time in bed." I waggle my brows when he faces me.

"Anyway," he replies, walking to the couch. "Work? Your parents are rich."

"Yes, but I'm not, and I'm not relying on them my whole life. I've done it enough already. They put money in accounts for me and Vi, but I'm still gonna have my own career, and working at Dad's old practice is good for me."

"What's up with Ro?"

"He's here on scholarship, but he works for everything else he needs." I pause. "Not everyone has their future secure like some people," I tease.

Dex shrugs, unaffected. His dad is the CEO and founder of a huge tech company, and Dex never has to worry about working if he doesn't want to, and if he does want a job, he can work for his dad at any time.

"Well, I'm gonna plan something fun for us to do, so I expect you two to take a weekend off and have fun with us."

"We're both off on weekends, so you're in luck."

"Good." He stands up. "Well, I guess I should head out."

"All right, man. See ya later."

Shortly after he leaves, Ronan comes in, and the look on his face makes me grin.

"I don't think it's fair that you got off early and decided to tease me by sending me that clip."

I fold my arms over my chest and cock my head. "Which clip was that?"

He drops his stuff on the table and stalks toward me. "Did you send many videos today?"

I may or may not have sent him a little video of me after I got out of the shower, and it may or may not have been NSFW, but it was thirty seconds at best.

"I was around people," he says, his fingers going for my button and zipper on my jeans. "You know how hard it was to act normal?"

Running my hand through his hair and giving it a little tug, I ask, "How hard was it?"

He bites down on his lip, pushing my jeans down. "Very hard."

"Mm."

Ronan drops to his knees in the middle of the living room

and takes my cock in his hand before sliding it between his lips and into his mouth.

"Oh fuck," I hiss, pulling on his hair again.

He sucks my dick like a pro, and I glance down, watching his lips stretch around my shaft. This visual is one I'll never get tired of.

His eyes flicker up and meet mine.

"Okay, let's go to the room. Now," I say.

I kick off my jeans and boxers where I stand, then pull off my shirt while I make my way down the hall. When I get to our room and turn around, I notice he's ridding himself of his clothes as well.

Both fully naked, I step forward and press my lips against his while my hands roam his toned body.

"I'm glad you got the message," I say, leaving his mouth to say those six words before I begin to kiss and nibble on his neck.

"I couldn't leave soon enough," he pants.

"I want to be inside you so bad."

"Give it to me, then," he replies in a low, husky voice.

I pull back and spin him around, bending him over the side of the bed. "Don't have to tell me twice."

After grabbing the lube and prepping him and slathering my cock in it, I position myself and slowly slide in.

"Fuck, baby," I grunt.

We switch fairly often, but I love fucking Ronan's ass, and I think he prefers it this way too.

"Yeah," he moans. "Fuck me."

He props one knee on the mattress and I grab a hold of his waist and move in and out. Faster. Harder. Deeper.

Ronan cries out in pleasure, his hand traveling to his cock, seeking a release.

"You gonna make a mess for me, baby?" I ask, my finger-tips digging into his flesh as I fuck him mercilessly.

"Yes. Oh yes!"

I let out a low growl as the muscles in his back flex. "I'm getting close."

"Oh, God!" he yells, his arm moving faster before his whole body spasms and tenses up. "Ahh. Oh shit. Yes."

Seconds later, and with a roar to startle the neighbors, I come deep inside of him. "Shi-it!" I say, the word breaking up as I gasp. What comes next is nothing but moans and grunts, and unintelligible noises that couldn't possibly be considered words.

I pull out slowly before falling to the bed in a sweaty heap.

Ronan moves to the other side to lay down. "We really need to start remembering to put a towel down. We've washed the covers like three times in ten days."

I chuckle. "I can't think right in the moment. My initial plan was to suck you off until you came in my mouth and then fuck you, but your ass is so addicting. It calls to me and I can't turn it down."

Ronan laughs. "You're crazy."

"I'm serious."

"I need to shower. Maybe I'll record a little video to send to you while you're at work. See how you like it."

"Oh, I'll like it very much."

"I'm sure you would."

He leans over to give me a quick peck, but I cradle his face and hold him there, deepening the kiss.

"You're amazing, you know that?" He blushes. "And I love you so fucking much it's crazy." Ronan opens his mouth to say something, but I stop him. "If you're about to say I'm *pretty okay*, I swear to God."

He throws his head back and laughs. "I wasn't." He grabs my chin, his face turning serious. "You're the best thing to ever happen to me, Lorenzo, and I'll love you always."

It's my turn to blush.

Prologue from Tasting Innocence

When: Six months ago
Where: Sleeping Bear Dunes Cabin
Situation: Stuck in a cabin with Vi while her parents are asleep. Alcohol has made me brave. Or stupid.

"I can't believe I'm stuck in this stupid cabin with you and my parents while Ronan is with Renzo," Violet complains.

"Come on, it's not that bad," I offer.

She makes a face. "Yeah, it is. I came here with Ronan and now he's stuck with my brother, who I think hates him. And I'm with my parents. *My parents*! Who knows how long we'll be snowed in."

I snort, knowing how Renzo feels about Ronan, and it's definitely not hatred. "Those two will be fine, and I don't think we'll be stuck for too long. They just have to clear the roads."

She rolls her eyes and spins around, heading for the kitchen, using her phone flashlight. "Hopefully the power comes back on soon."

"I'm sure it will. I'll start a fire, though. Then we can get drunk by the fireplace."

"Drunk?" she questions, eyeing me carefully before dropping her voice. "You have liquor?"

"Yep," I answer with a smirk.

"Give me some."

My thoughts go elsewhere with that statement. I've been quietly and secretly lusting after my best friend's sister for a year now. With each passing day she gets more beautiful, and she's one of the coolest chicks I know.

"It's in the car, as well as your brother's bag. He's gonna be pissed when he realizes he doesn't have any of his clothes."

She shrugs. "He'll live."

After I fight through the wind and snow just to get to the car to grab my bag, I come back in to find the power's back on and Violet's texting away on her phone.

"You okay?" she asks, not looking at me.

"Yeah, the fucking wind is terrible, and the snow's really coming down. Your mom might've been right about it being like this tomorrow."

I shake snow from my hair as I remove my jacket and boots, and then reach into the duffle bag and clutch the neck of the bottle of Jack Daniels.

"Still want that drink?" I ask her.

"Definitely. Do we have anything to mix it with, though? I'm not too experienced with liquor."

I go to the fridge, grateful her parents had it in mind to grab some food beforehand. "Coke okay?"

"That works. I'm just texting Ronan. I'll be in there in a minute."

I bite down my annoyed groan. It's not that Ronan is a bad guy, but I hate that he's with Violet. And on a Christmas break trip? They haven't even known each other that long.

After I make our drinks, we go to the living room and

plop down on the couch and turn the TV on. I'm aware of every movement she makes, and any time I think of saying something stupid like *I really like you* or *you're so beautiful* or *I want to kiss you*, I take a drink. Eventually, I drink enough to give me the liquid courage I shouldn't have right now.

While we watch some show I'm not even paying attention to, I allow my knee to fall onto hers. I notice her stiffen briefly, but she doesn't move. Instead, she turns and stares right at me. All I can do is give her a small smirk.

Another half hour goes by, and she starts getting a little buzzed—laughing at the sitcom, but when she laughs, she places her hand on my knee.

It's nothing, I know that, but God do I want it to be. If Renzo knew the things I was thinking about right now, he'd kill me.

Violet gets up to go to the kitchen, making another drink for herself. "You want more?" she asks.

"Yeah."

I stand up and walk in behind her, stopping too close. When I lean over to pour the watered down remnants of my drink into the sink, my crotch touches her ass and I nearly moan at the sensation. Fucking alcohol always makes me horny, and it's not like I need much help. I'm a twenty-year-old guy for Christ's sake.

Violet angles her head over her shoulder and narrows her eyes at me, but I shrug. So stupid. She's probably gonna end up hating me before the night's over.

"So what do you see in Ronan?" I ask.

"What?"

"Why do you like him?"

"Uhh, because he's hot and nice."

"You're not the only one who thinks that," I say with a chuckle.

"What do you mean? Who else thinks that?"

"Your brother," I answer, taking another sip. "He's probably thrilled to be locked up with him."

She nearly spits out her drink. "What?" A drunken laugh slips between her lips. "Renzo likes Ronan? Is that why he's been such a dick lately?"

My eyes feel heavy as I grin. "I don't know. I guess."

"Oh my God!" she squeals, scrambling for her phone.

Shit, I guess the alcohol has my lips a little too loose.

As she texts who I can only assume is her brother, I head to the bathroom. I splash water on my face, staring at my reflection in the mirror. I tell myself not to do anything else. I've really pushed the limits with touching her and flirting like she isn't my best friend's sister, but the alcohol has already taken effect, and all I can think about is spilling my guts to her. So what, she came here with her boyfriend? He doesn't know her like I do. We have history.

Her voice carries down the hall, letting me know she's now talking on the phone. Fuck, I hope Renzo isn't pissed that I spilled about his crush.

I eventually head back into the living room and spot Violet in the kitchen rinsing out the glasses.

"Everything okay?"

She nods, a small grin on her lips. "Yep."

"Is Zo pissed that I told you?"

She laughs. "He doesn't get mad about much. He was honest. He thinks Ro's hot, which I get."

He'd get mad if I did all the things I'm thinking about doing to his sister right now.

"You going to bed?" I ask.

"Yeah, I'm just hiding evidence."

Fuck. My time is coming to an end.

"Okay. I guess I'll crash too," I say, turning the TV off. When she saunters into the living room, I grin. "I'll walk you to your room."

She rolls her eyes and makes a noise in the back of her throat. "You're weird."

My warring thoughts and feelings ping pong around in my brain, and I fight with what I want to do versus what I should do. Or shouldn't in this case.

At her door, she gives me a strange look, probably wondering why I'm being weird.

"Well...goodnight."

She hesitates, and something in her eyes gives me the courage to lean in. Before my lips can touch her, I see her move back just a fraction, so I change course and end up just kissing her on the cheek.

"Goodnight."

Violet stares at me, shock written on her face, so I quickly turn and go to my room, cursing myself the whole way there.

I thought I saw interest and curiosity in her eyes before. As she realized what I was about to do, she probably freaked out. My drunken gaze misread the whole thing, and now I have to deal with the awkwardness that'll follow. Maybe I can get her to talk to me tomorrow. She probably thinks it's just because I've been drinking, but that's not true.

I want her, and I've never wanted anyone like this before.

Acknowledgments

I want to thank you, yes you, for reading my book. It still baffles me that people are interested in my words, so thank you for picking this up and giving it a chance.

My cover artist, Robin, is owed a huge thanks for always creating magic and dealing with me through the process. You're the best! Thanks for making this, and the others, so perfect.

Tiffany, thanks for proofing my words and helping polish it up.

Cass! You're new to my team, but I couldn't have done this without you. Thanks for the teasers, the encouraging words, and all the help with the ARC team and release.

I couldn't do this without my beta readers for catching the problems and plot holes, and little things that just didn't make sense. Thanks for letting me know that someone grabbed a condom but didn't put it on. Haha! Kizzy, Cass, Krystal, and Elizabeth—you're the best.

Thank you to Candi Kane for doing another stellar job on my cover reveal and blitz for this and the ones to come!

Bloggers, bookstagrammers, reviewers, and new on the block—booktokkers! Thanks for your excitement, time, reviews, pictures, videos, and posts! You're the real heroes!

And I can't forget to thank my husband, who's always there to listen and help. Thanks for your support and love! You're my everything!